Women's Voices

Stephanie!
Congratulations!
on Graduation! Here's
a book of you. Here's
your Graduation gift,
Enjoy the characters
More to come...

Love,
Rebekah S Cole

Cousin Becky
2016

A novel by

Rebekah S. Cole

Cover design by Justin Q. Young

Printed in the United States of America
First Edition
ISBN: 1478255048
ISBN 9781478255048

Library of Congress Control Number:
2016902012
CreateSpace Indepentdent Publishing Platform
North Charleston, South Carolina

For my two heartbeats: Lexy and Nadi.
All things are possible, if you only believe...

For my grammy, Henrietta June Anderson Mitchell, (1923-2000)
These women's voices needed to be heard.

The Gifts

By Rebekah S. Cole

A special hearty meal
Nurturing during a time to heal
That fragrance only you can wear
A unique bond that only we can share
… Thank you mother

Hand in hand, side by side
With you only I will confide
Sharing secrets with a giggle and a hush
Defending and protecting like you do so much
…Thank you sister

A helping hand, a lending ear
Through tough challenges and facing fears
Dancing through the night 'til we sweat
Oh, I'm so glad that we met
… Thank you friend

Upon first sight love cannot be denied
In your world I am mesmerized
Inside and out watching you grow
Teaching you everything you should know
… Thank you daughter

Author's Note...

This novel is a labor of love and a work of pure fiction. While these family issues portrayed in each relationship may be relatable, they are derived from my imagination. Neither the characters nor any situations that occur in this story should be construed as real. This fictional family, like most, is a work in progress as they work towards redemption. Now, turn the pages and escape from your family drama into theirs.

1

Colette

"**I** certainly hope this is your last baby," her mother, Jonetta, admonished. She was holding Colette's newest daughter, Delilah, who was undeniably adorable at just six weeks old. This was baby number four for Colette. And her mother was all but happy about it.

"Don't worry mother," Colette sighed. "I got my tubes tied this time."

"Good!" Her mother exclaimed and continued. "You would think that you learned your lesson the last time Owen went upside your head for getting pregnant the third time. But, no, you had to go and have another baby adding to your burdens. Are you trying to run your man away?"

Colette stared at the floor biting back tears. Her mother always had a way of making her feel like she had made the worst decision right after she gave birth. It's not like she was a single woman having babies by random men. She was married to Owen Aldridge, the love of her life. But her mother never approved of him. Colette was love struck and barely made it out of high school. Her only interest was being with Owen, who was five years older than she was and had his own apartment. To her mother's horror, Colette moved in with him and immediately became pregnant when she was only nineteen-years-old.

Her mother insisted that Owen should make an honest woman out of her before she started to show. Owen, being an independent man - who did not take kindly to any woman telling him what to do - made it clear that he would marry her when he was good and ready. They eventually married, in their own time, but in her third trimester Colette suffered a miscarriage losing their first baby. The doctors did not have any explanations other than the baby seemed healthy but decided to come out too soon. But Colette knew it more likely that it was because Owen pushed her and held her down on the floor when they were fighting at the time.

They may not have been the ideal couple, but she was certain that Owen loved her and their children. Anybody who wanted to claim otherwise could kick rocks, as far as Colette was concerned. Colette was on the defense for sure now. She flicked her braid over her shoulder and straightened her posture.

"Owen didn't beat me because I got pregnant, mama. He was just frustrated about not having enough money to support another baby. Owen doesn't even hit me anymore. Besides, it's not like I'm getting pregnant by myself!" Colette felt compelled to explain. "I can't help it if my husband can't keep his hands off of me."

"In what way?" Jonetta scoffed. "From the looks of things you get more black eyes around here than love."

"You *know* what I meant, mama," Colette glared at her mother and hoped she would change the subject.

"Well, I have no idea why you refused to get on birth control all these years. It would've done you some good, but too bad, you missed the memo on that one." Jonetta rolled her eyes at Colette. "But, truth be told, you should've been on birth control after the second baby. You had a boy and then a girl. What more could you ask for? You always were greedy." Jonetta lit a cigarette with one hand, turned her face from blowing smoke directly on the baby, took a few puffs and continued. "Now look at you. At first, you had trouble even carrying a baby, having miscarriages and all. You lost your girlish figure in between. Then you just start spitting these kids out like a rabbit. You'll never get that body back, girl. The only reason I had three children is because I got stuck with two girls being born first. I promise you if it wasn't for your father being adamant about having a boy, I would've had my tubes tied right after you were born. That's the truth! And look what happened... ended up with another girl anyway on the third-go-round. Dawn better be glad she's cute." Jonetta shook her head and took another pull from her cigarette. "Speaking of the devil, has your father even called to say he would visit his new granddaughter yet?"

Colette sighed. "No, mama, but I'm sure he will soon."

"No surprise there. Norman always was a self-centered bastard!" Jonetta declared, rolling her eyes. Divorced now for 30 years and still her mother never could find a kind word to say about her father, Norman Miller.

"Babies are a blessing from God," Georgia said emerging from the kitchen with grilled cheese sandwiches on a tray. Georgia was the oldest and only sister that her mother had. She decided that today would be a good time to visit Colette as well. Colette always welcomed her Aunt Georgia; she always made everything seem alright.

"Thank you very much, Aunt Georgia," Colette agreed.

Georgia continued. "They are sweet and perfect gifts. I certainly wish I could have given Fred a few, but God didn't see fit."

"Don't encourage her, Georgia. She needs to understand that having babies is not the way to keep a man," Jonetta said, pacing the floor patting her granddaughter on the back hoping she would burp soon. "It's a recipe for just the opposite if you ask me. Men are not made to handle children and all the responsibility that comes along with it. Our father is a good example of that."

"Not all men are like our father, Netta. I'm sure Owen is doing the best he can and he hasn't gone anywhere," Georgia said, giving Colette an encouraging pat on the knee as she sat beside her on the musty, threadbare sofa.

"Not yet. But actually, he would probably be doing you a favor if he did disappear." Jonetta raised her eyebrows like she had a plan. "You could get more government assistance if he wasn't around. I told you not to get involved with those Aldridge boys, but no, you didn't want to listen to me. They're all a bunch of good-for-nothings."

"Mama, please!" Colette had enough finally.

"Norman is a good man, though," Georgia added, winking at her sister.

"Oh, please!" Jonetta retorted. She flicked her wrist and ashes from her cigarette fell to the floor.

"Well, I'm so glad God blessed you to have children, sugar. It must be a wonderful feeling to see your children's faces. Fred always wanted lots of children. He would have made a wonderful father, I just know it." Georgia tried to peaceably change the subject. She was always taking the moral high road.

"Well, I guess you'll never know," Jonetta retorted. She hated her sister's pleasant disposition. She certainly wasn't that pleasant while they were growing up together. It was quite the contrary as a matter-of-fact. Georgia was always very stingy with her things, always hiding them. That peach frolic dress was their undoing and it changed Jonetta's life forever. Listening to Georgia now it seemed like she moved away and became a brainwashed Stepford wife. Maybe she had to be this way because she had a white husband.

Colette gave her mother a disapproving look. "Mama, give me my baby," she demanded with her arms outstretched. Jonetta obliged even though she had not gotten the baby to burp.

"She's going to have colic," Jonetta warned and took a long drag from her cigarette.

"I should be heading home," Georgia announced and kissed both of her nieces on the forehead. "Please let me know if you ever need to babysit your beautiful children, okay sugar? I'm just a phone call away. Too bad I missed the other children on this visit. I was certainly looking forward to all those hugs and kisses."

Colette looked at her aunt apologetically, but Georgia returned a sympathetic look for Colette. After all, she was the one stuck with a cruel mother and a violent husband. Only God could help her situation.

"Yes, I suppose it is time for Fred to eat dinner. He can't seem to make a move without you around," Jonetta said sarcastically as she walked her sister to the front door which was only about five steps away from the sofa.

"That's not true," Georgia contested. "Fred just prefers to watch me make my moves."

Georgia and Colette shared a laugh.

"Yeah, well, make sure you take good care of that man because there are plenty of women that will gladly slide right on in and take your place," Jonetta remarked.

Georgia laughed at her younger sister's so-called advice on men. Colette watched as her Aunt Georgia kept her composure as she tied the leather belt around her camel-colored trench coat. She had such grace and class.

"The last thing I'm concerned about is another woman replacing me. I doubt if any woman could ever fill my shoes. Besides, Fred stays satisfied in every way imaginable. He'll be happy to tell you all about it next time. All you have to do is ask, Netta."

Jonetta forced a smile and bid her sister a good-bye closing the door quickly behind her. She exhaled as she walked back to the sofa and declared, "Sometimes I wish she never moved up here. It's not like she's been any use to us. She just flaunts around in all her fancy clothes." Jonetta pranced around mocking Georgia's walk. She mashed her cigarette down in a metal ashtray.

Colette shook her head and decided to ignore her mother's blatant jealousy. Instead, she asked, "Since when did you become such an expert on men?"

"I know a thing or two, missy. How do you think you got here?" Jonetta asked rhetorically as she sat next to Colette and flipped through a two-month-old Essence magazine.

"So daddy was your first and only man?" Colette asked already knowing the answer to that question. But after the way her mother had been making her feel worthless all afternoon, she wanted to get underneath her skin.

They exchanged a long glare.

"That's none of your business," Jonetta admonished. "But I can tell you that when I was your age, being a mother was the last thing on my mind. There is a whole big world out there and you've wasted a good part of your twenties trying to be a wife to a violent drunk! And now you're a thirty-two-year old mother to four helpless children. "

"Those children were the *only* grandchildren you had at one time," Colette countered. "Phyllis couldn't get pregnant to save her life, now she has twins, miraculously. Dawn is too busy traveling this 'whole big world' that you speak of and she's probably never coming back. Actually, you should be grateful that my children are filling a void in your life. What would you be doing otherwise, mama? I mean... other than trying to steal your sister's husband."

Colette had overstepped her boundaries and she knew it. Her mother's nostrils flared and she was mashing her perfectly painted red lips together repeatedly.

Jonetta stood over Colette and wagged her finger in her face.

"We'll see if you're so quick to be disrespectful the next time you need some help around here." Jonetta said, eyeing her daughter's apartment with disgust. "Contrary to popular belief, I have better things to do than to sit around here in this filthy place."

And with that, her mother finally left without even saying good-bye.

"Good riddance to her," Colette said and kissed her daughter's forehead. "Your grandmother is such a bitch. But that's just between me and you, okay?"

Colette nuzzled her nose underneath her baby's chin and inhaled deeply, she loved the way newborns smelled. She smiled warmly at her daughter and placed her gently in the hand-me-down crib that seemed to be a permanent fixture in their tiny dining area over the past five years. Each time she thought to have Owen remove it, she found that she was pregnant again.

At one point Ruthie and Lydia were sharing the crib because they were so close in age and quite frankly there had not been any other option. She scanned the apartment looking for the "filth" that her mother described, but only found a few toys out of place which was normal around there. A few dishes in the sink, and maybe the floors needed to be swept, but nothing major. Nevertheless, she gathered the toys and tossed them in the girls' room just in case Owen wanted to harp on the same issue once he returned with the kids.

Colette sucked her teeth now looking at the untouched grilled cheese sandwiches her Aunt Georgia made. She was being a thoughtful busy body, as usual, but nonetheless, Owen would not be happy about food being wasted. It was already hard to come by and throwing away food was not an option in their household. "Waste not. Want not." She could hear her mother saying in the back of her mind.

Colette bit into the now stiffening, cheese that was once gooey, fresh out of the skillet. She caught a glance of herself in the mirror hanging on the wall between the living room and dining area and let out a dis-appointing sigh. Her sandy brown hair flowed past her shoulders. But these days it was easier to keep it in a single braid because she had tod-dlers to chase after. Colette used to have smooth, flawless skin until it suffered from pregnancy-induced acne, even though it didn't take away from her beauty, she felt otherwise. Her big brown eyes won the hearts of many, but she only had eyes for Owen.

He was tall, built like a husky football player, although he nev-er played any sport. The only sport he knew well was how to seduce a woman, and he was good at it. Although he accused Colette of being with other men, Owen was Colette's first and only sexual experience. And according to her, it was mind blowing sex. Owen had a Puerto Rican mother who married an average looking black man, but all of the Aldridge brothers came out with a fair complexion sporting black, wavy hair. The Aldridge clan had the looks, charm, and just enough bad-boy charisma that got most impressionable girls into trouble. Colette was one of them.

A feeling of guilt overcame her as she swallowed the bite of grilled cheese. Colette hurried past the mirror. Her mother was right, Colette had gained a lot of weight between each baby, and her double chin was proof enough of that. The last thing she should be doing was eating a heavily buttered grilled cheese sandwich, but she didn't want Owen to fuss and possibly hit her for being so wasteful. The other sandwiches she would save for the kids to snack on later, she decided.

Where were they anyway? Owen took their other three children to the library for an arts and crafts event with some of the local artists. It was free and it was something to do other than have the kids keeping up noise in the cramped apartment on a Saturday afternoon. The library had closed an hour ago. It certainly did not take another hour just to get home from the library. But Colette closed her eyes and mindlessly took another bite of the sandwich. She welcomed the silence that occupied the space in the apartment.

The sound of elephants trampling up the hallway stairs forced her eyelids to flick open. Her brood was home and everyone in the building knew it. Colette reluctantly walked to the door to let them in, but not before she made them aware that their baby sister, Delilah, was sleeping. But for whatever reason they couldn't keep their excitement down to a hush. When Owen appeared in the doorway, he too had a foolish grin on his face.

"Well, what's everyone so giddy about?" She questioned with her hand on her hip.

Owen kissed her forehead and closed the door behind him. "I hit the lottery, baby!" he exclaimed and picked up Colette slightly from where she stood. He realized she was too heavy to swing around like he wanted to and quickly put her down. "I took the kids to that new McDonald's for dinner as a celebration."

"Really? How much did you win?" Colette raised her eyebrows expectantly waiting for more details.

"Well, I didn't hit the jackpot or no shit like that," Owen admitted. "But winning this two hundred dollars sure will put us in the black for a few weeks." He walked over to the crib to peek at his newborn daughter who was still sleeping peacefully. Delilah had become accustomed to the Aldridge clan raucous.

Although Colette was annoyed by Owen's cursing and gambling vernacular in front of the children, she smiled as he probably expected her to do, but she was not impressed by a measly two-hundred dollars that would probably be spent before the end of the week on his poison of choice. But clearly Owen was happy, if only for a little while and she was relieved that she didn't have to prepare dinner tonight.

"So everyone's bellies should be full then?"

"Daddy bought us ice cream too!" Lydia volunteered. Just at five-years-old she was already very bright and everyone noticed. She was not going to be left out of the conversation by any means. Colette often told her that she would one day grow up and become a news reporter.

"Is that right?" Colette teased and bent down to pinch her daughter's cheeks.

"Yeah, but we had cheeseburgers and French fries first," Cornell said matter-of-factly. "I ate all of mine!" He rubbed his belly smiling at his father for confirmation that it was good and he appreciated the treat. Cornell was always animated, but being the oldest of the Aldridge tribe just at seven-years-old, he was proving to be very responsible.

"Mommy, we saw Wonna McDonna too!" Ruthie chimed in pulling at Colette's tattered housecoat. Ruthie always needed so much attention, but Colette expected that of her three-year-old. Sometimes Owen and Ruthie acted so much alike that there could never be any doubt that he was her father based on their actions alone.

Owen stood boasting like he just won the Heavy Weight Championship belt. Colette was glad that he was in a good mood, though. It was very rare to see him smile and show some pride. She looked at him quizzically, "Ronald McDonald was there?"

He shrugged and smiled, "Just so happens it was our luck that he was there greeting customers today. I'm telling you, babe, it's been a lucky day all around. The kids had a good time at the library too," he reached into his back pack to pull out their colorful drawings and paintings. The kids crowded him to get their paintings and show their mom which one was theirs.

"And nobody thought to call me in the all this fun?"

"That government phone ain't worth nothing. They cut it off today. Your phone should be dead too by now."

She was not happy with that news at all. He couldn't pay a bill on time if someone paid him to do it. Although Owen held the same job as a garbage man in Streets and Sanitation over the past ten years, it never seemed to be enough money to go around, which made for endless arguments especially during one of his drunken rages. But he was her man, and she loved him.

"I'll tell you what," Colette said to the children. "I'm going to frame each one of these. But for now, calm down, go wash up because some of you are sticky, and let me talk to daddy for a minute."

The kids obeyed still all smiles. Colette decided not to inquire any further about their cell phones being cut off and instead gave Owen a seductive smile. She embraced him and planted a kiss on his cheek, "So you deserve the daddy of the year award, huh?"

"Had it not been for this lucky hit, it would've been just a regular old damn day," he gushed. "I feel like I'm on top of the world!"

"It was a stroke of luck," she agreed. "But how far will it carry us? Can we get our phones cut back on, at least?"

He pulled her arms from around his neck with a frown and held her stare, "Like I said I didn't hit the jackpot, but damn, it's better than nothing! Why can't you just live in the damn moment?"

Not wanting to start an argument, she smoothed his face with her hand, "I'm happy for you, I really am. The kids are so..."

"Get off of me," Owen snatched away from her and headed to the kitchen. She heard the refrigerator door being yanked open, then the opening of a beer can.

Colette peered around the corner at him and tried again, "Baby, thank you for making this day special for the kids. I love seeing all of your faces light up like that."

Owen grunted and took another swallow of beer, then wiped his mouth with the back of his hand. "Don't you even wanna know which numbers I played?" He asked annoyed.

Colette nodded, "Which ones?"

"The day I met you combined with your birthday," he said almost in disbelief. He reached down in his pants pocket and pulled out the receipt to show her. "See, there?" He pointed at the numbers. "I never thought these damn numbers would hit. I almost gave up playing them since I've been playing the same ones for years."

"Have you, baby?" Colette stood behind him and massaged his shoulders. She wondered how much money he had spent over the years playing the lottery. One thing was for sure it was more than the two-hundred dollars that he just won. But instead, she replied, "That's so sweet of you. We have to celebrate!"

"What the hell you think I've been doing all day?" he retorted. "Me and the kids already started. When are you going to stop being such a damn killjoy and join in on the fun?" Owen turned to grab her by the arm and Colette flinched. She thought he was about to hit her for sure.

Owen grinned at her needless fear this time and pulled her closer to tongue kiss her passionately while caressing her plump butt.

"I wanna have some fun with you too," he said and quickly glided his hands to his favorite part of a woman's body. Owen cupped her small breasts that were full of milk. "I love your tits full like this," he whispered in her ear and gently squeezed them. Milk saturated the front of her t-shirt, but that turned him on even more. He untied her house coat, lifted her t-shirt to get a full view of her breasts, and squeezed them harder this time. He quickly licked the streaming milk from her breasts like he did not want to waste a drop.

He moaned and smacked his lips. "This shit tastes better than any milkshake I've ever had." Owen greedily continued to swallow his newborn daughter's meal.

Owen had a thing for her breast milk. He had told Colette after their first child, Cornell, was born that her breasts belonged to him whenever he wanted them and babies were only on borrowed time. In the middle of the night, she would sometimes be awakened by a strong pull on her nipple. Colette knew that it was her husband getting his "midnight snack", as he called it. Owen claimed that he liked the sweet taste of her milk and preferred that size on her rather than her normal B cup.

Whenever Owen grew tired of his breast milk fetish he would let her know for sure. But until then, this caused her breasts to stay full of milk much longer than she had liked. To be more exact, it was going on two years now that she had milk in her breasts. The doctor offered Colette pills that would dry it up, but she refused because she didn't want to anger Owen. At times, they became sore and cracked, but the more Colette protested the longer he would indulge just to prove to her that he was in control of her body, so she learned after giving birth to Lydia to just let him have his way.

Now she felt him rise through his pants and he was pressing hard against her pelvis.

"You feel that?" Owen asked licking his lips.

Owen was always so impatient after she had a baby. He never did want to wait over a month to make love to her again, but this time, Colette insisted that he wait until the six-week checkup. Delilah just had an appointment earlier in the week, and so did she. Her doctor approved of regular sex again. But she did not share the news with Owen. She knew that he didn't need the doctor's approval because he was going to have his way regardless. His sex drive was in full force over the past five years and she had the children to prove it. And her mother wondered why she kept getting pregnant so quickly? She couldn't keep her man off of her!

Since it had been over a decade since the last time her mother had any sex Colette figured that she was just jealous of their active sex life. Quite frankly, she was grateful that Owen still wanted to be intimate with her in spite of the 30-pound weight gain. After all, it was her wifely duty. Furthermore, Colette certainly didn't want him to go find pleasure elsewhere.

"Turn around," Owen ordered. "I want some now."

"The kids may walk in here and see us!" Colette tried to protest as he forced her to turn around.

"This will be quick," he reassured Colette. "I've waited long enough. I'm about to fuckin' explode in my pants, now bend over and grab your ankles, girl."

Colette did as she was told even though she knew it would be a messy sight to see once he was done. She was grateful that he was in a good mood though and having sex with her would be the icing on the cake for the remainder of the night. He would probably even want more sex later. Regardless of what her mother thought about her husband, they had plenty of good times together. And it was turning out to be a good day.

2

Phyllis

When Phyllis thought of her husband Damien, the first thing that came to mind was that crooked smile and his beautiful sandy brown locs that have grown to his shoulders. Damien came into her life at the best time in the worst of her twenties. He saved her from a dead-end relationship with a loser who was playing with her mind, time and emotions. That fool was never going to marry her.

Phyllis met Damien at Chicago's annual Chosen Few picnic in July. He was already in a relationship with one of their mutual friends at the time. Needless to say, their relationship did not last long once Phyllis and Damien exchanged numbers. Phyllis didn't believe that a man could be stolen from another woman. On the contrary, she believed that a woman couldn't keep a man that didn't want to be kept. After a few dates, and constantly talking on the phone, they were inseparable. They did not care who disapproved of the thirteen year age difference, nor about the friendships that they lost over it. When Damien proposed a year later, she accepted. Even though her mother always advised to never marry the first man who proposes, Phyllis didn't regret it.

The only times she questioned her decision is when they had money troubles and trouble conceiving, but the twins, Serena and Sabrina, were here now. The money troubles have been off and on for the past seven years. She didn't know what they were going to do. It was always something. If it wasn't their car being repossessed, it was the lights being cut off. If it wasn't that then it was late payments on the rent and begging the landlord to be patient with them. It wasn't like this before the twins were born, but now they had to pay double for everything since they've been born.

Sometimes Phyllis wished that she would have listened to her mother because maybe she would not feel stuck in a penniless marriage. But she would never admit that to her mother because she would only gloat at being right.

Phyllis used to work at a litigation firm for almost ten years but refused to have the twins raised by a daycare provider. Sabrina and Serena were her babies that she prayed for and desperately wanted so badly. Nobody was going to have a hand in raising them. Besides, after she did the math, her whole check would be going straight to the daycare center anyway. She made the decision to quit her job to take care of their two-month-old babies without discussing it with Damien. She knew better than to make such a major decision without her husband's input, but she also knew that he would try to convince her to continue to work. Phyllis figured he made enough money to keep them afloat... or so she thought. Sure, Damien was pissed about it, but it was done.

Since neither one of them are financially responsible, they do not play the blame game. They both spend the money as soon as they got it in their hands. Phyllis loved to shop either in stores, online or by watching the Home Shopping Network. Although she had not looked at one of Damien's pay stubs in years, she still figured that it should be enough to take care of a family of four. Yet, they struggled to make ends meet. It just didn't make sense to her.

Damien may not have known how to budget properly, but he still knew how to turn her on even though he was 48-years-old, she reasoned. He erased all of her doubts and fears when they made love. It's like their problems magically disappeared in those moments until the phone rang or they got a bill in the mail. The problem this week is their landlord notified them that they have to move out by the end of the month. Phyllis tried to suppress her resentment and anger rising, but she knew that the seams were coming loose. She refused to beg her divorced mother for help because she was on one income just like them, but it was Damien's job to take care of them. Even though her mother didn't have any major expenses anymore, and could probably afford to lend money, Phyllis didn't want her - or anyone for that matter - knowing just how bad their situation was at this point.

Asking her dad for help was out of the question because being the southern man that he is, believed strongly that grown men should not allow their women to go around asking for help. He even suggested that Phyllis return to work, but she reassured him that was not going to happen anytime soon. Although her dad is cordial to Damien when they got together as a family she could tell that he really didn't care for him. This was exactly why Phyllis had not told a soul about their dilemma yet because it was too embarrassing and stressful. Most of their friends thought that they owned their house, but her family knew better.

Phyllis wished she could click her brain off to stop thinking. It was nice and quiet in her home, but all of that was about to change in an hour when the twins got home from school. Phyllis sat in Damien's recliner with a nice cold Corona and a bag of movie theater flavored microwaved popcorn, kicked her feet up and decided to catch up on her reality shows. "The Real Housewives" of anyplace was her favorite guilty pleasure. Phyllis thought the title was ridiculous because the majority of women on the show were not even married.

"I'm a *real* housewife, but I don't keep up half the mess that you do!" Phyllis yelled to the television. Today she decided to catch up on the New Jersey cast.

Phyllis picked up her smartphone to post on Facebook about the foolishness, but the phone rang flashing Damien's face. She sucked her teeth and clicked the pause button on the remote. She was not in the mood to talk to him. Phyllis knew that he was only going to ask her a thousand questions about the search for a new place, or he was going to ask about dinner or want her to do something. She finally answered after the fourth ring.

"Hey, babe," Phyllis said trying to sound cheerful.

"What are you doing?" he quizzed with authority.

"What do you think I'm doing?" She snapped at him. There was a time that his voice used to make her feel all tingly inside. Now it just irritated the hell out of her.

"Probably nothing," he chuckled. "Or posting on Facebook, or watching your reality shows, or putting pictures of the twins all over Instagram. Yeah, basically, nothing."

She took a swig of beer. "Well, I'll have you know that I'm sweeping the kitchen. That's why it took so long for me to answer," she lied.

"Did you get a chance to look online at some rental homes?" He asked anxiously.

Phyllis sighed. She knew that he was calling to bother her about that. She swore Damien was worse than a nagging wife. He gets them into hot water, and then expected Phyllis to jump through hoops to get them out of it. Damien expected her to do the new house hunting of course because he figured that she sat around all day on her hands. Their five-year-old, Kindergarten twins kept her busy as soon as they hit the door in the afternoon. Phyllis also volunteered at their school, attended field trips, provided most of the goodies for all the bake sales, and led the annual fundraiser. Those are definitely jobs according to Phyllis. Finding a new home to rent also means finding a new school district if they could not find a home in their current neighborhood. She could not imagine who would even give them a chance with their horrible financial track record. Certainly their landlord wouldn't be a good reference. Phyllis would have to put down someone's information when asked for references. They wouldn't know the difference anyway.

"Yes, but I didn't see anything that interests me in this area," she lied again. She had not even touched the laptop today. "How's your day going?" Phyllis asked to change the subject quickly.

"Same as usual. Same route, same faces, same shit, different day," Damien grunted.

Phyllis could tell that he was rubbing his beard because she heard that rustling scraping noise. He only did that when he was pondering something or nervous about something. Lately, Damien had not been shaving. He grew a full beard and let his locs grow longer than usual. Phyllis liked the rough and rugged look, but his hair was so coarse that it scraped her when he hugged her, nuzzled his head on her neck or pleasured her in her hot spot. She could see if he was keeping it lined up tastefully, but he's just letting his beard grow wild like a caveman.

"But listen, sweets, I talked to old man Wilkerson, and he said that he would give us forty-five days. That's an extension of two weeks."

"I can add," she retorted and rolled her eyes.

"But we still need to get a move on this, sweets," Damien replied. He always called her "sweets" when he wanted her to do something for him. He just used it twice. Damien could try to butter her up all he wanted, but it wasn't working on Phyllis this time. It was just a precursor for a request: cleaning, cooking his favorite meal, running an errand, and even sex. "We have to start packing, so I'm bringing home boxes today from the warehouse. We can start with packing books and other shit we don't use on a regular daily basis."

See, there it was. A request. "That's funny that you keep saying 'we' when you know good and damn well that I'm going to be the one doing all of the packing!"

"Well, that's just the price you have to pay since *you* chose to be a housewife. It's not like you have anything better to do," Damien snapped back.

Phyllis gasped. She could not believe her ears. He still had not gotten over the fact that she quit her job without consulting him. That was five years ago, but he still had not gotten over it.

"Look, my break is almost over. I'll see you when I get home... with the boxes." Damien ended the call without even as much as a good-bye.

Phyllis was too outdone. "He better not even think about hugging, kissing, nor sexing me today," she said aloud.

She had twenty more minutes of peace and quiet before the school bus dropped the girls off. Phyllis took another a sip of beer but decided that was not going to be enough. She headed to the basement where they kept the hard liquor at the bar. They rarely used the space down there unless it was to entertain for the Super Bowl or the basketball championship games. It was such a well-remodeled basement. Old man Wilkerson had done a superb job rehabbing this house. Phyllis had furnished the basement with leather sofas, a 60-inch flat screen, bar stools, and decorated the bathroom. Damien liked the way she furnished it but complained that she spent way too much money on a space that they rarely used. Well, the whole idea was to make it look nice enough for them to want to use it. After all, this was their home and Phyllis made it into a welcoming home, but now they have to move due to late payments. Damien was not doing something right financially. It just didn't add up.

The bottle of vodka was calling her name. Phyllis turned the bottle up and felt the sting go down. She squinted and coughed from the aftermath. Her cheeks flushed. She took one more sip because that would help her to handle whatever came through the door today.

3

Dawn

Dawn was so tired of the night sweats that she began sleeping with the fan on. Which annoyed Vine, her boyfriend, but he learned to deal with it and her recurring nightmares. He encouraged her to see a therapist about it, but she refused. Dawn maintained that seeing herself as a child and watching a withered, old white woman being smothered to death in her dreams was enough for her imagination. She believed that a therapist would only incite more nightmares or even worse reveal that it might have actually happened. For now the fan, smoking weed and drinking Shiraz before bed would just have to do.

She made a mental note to mention the nightmares to her mother. Maybe there was something to it, maybe not. Dawn knew that it was best to mention the nightmares once she was back at home for Thanksgiving. Otherwise, her mother would just worry about her being so far away. God could actually take a nap if He wanted to because Jonetta seemed to be on duty twenty-four-seven with worry.

By the time she graduated from high school Dawn knew that she wanted to become a fashion model. Never one for really following the rules, being the baby of the family and all, nobody was surprised at all when Dawn refused to attend college. She felt that an education institution couldn't teach her about what came naturally. She landed her first job within three months in a print ad for Macy's. Dawn also became the young, fresh face at Fashion Fair cosmetics and did runway shows in Chicago, L.A., New York, Atlanta and D.C. Her mother swore that when Dawn was a toddler she couldn't get her from in front of a mirror. She was wearing Barbie heels, boas, and putting on shows for the family at every function.

It's no wonder that she was totally in love with an actor. Dawn was very positive about Vine Clarke making it in this business. He already had done commercials for Old Navy, JCPenney and Sprite. Vine was one to watch and Dawn was going to be right in the lime light with him when he made it.

Their studio apartment in New York was probably as big as a walk-in closet, but it was a great location for Vine to get to his Off-Broadway show, *Stomp*. He was an understudy now, but Dawn was certain that he would have his big break sooner than later. Vine had a knack for impersonating voices like Forrest Whitaker, President Barack Obama and President Bill Clinton, and the funniest impression of Arnold Schwarzenegger. That's actually how they met three years ago. There was a local play at Chicago State University in the dead, middle of a bitter winter, but she promised her friend, Chena, that she would attend with her if she bought the tickets and drove. Chena had a cousin who was co-producer of the play and they were advertising all over Facebook and the radio about it. Naturally, Dawn had to support it even though it was at Chena's expense.

Thanks to Chicago's efficient transit system and cab service, Dawn didn't own a car. Chena picked her up from Jonetta's house and it was snowing like there was no tomorrow, then the flurries stopped suddenly as they drove slowly. That was typical bipolar Chicago weather.

In Act Two there he was a tall chocolate drop portraying an abusive lover who suffered from PTSD. Vine played that role so well that he had the audience on an emotional roller coaster. One minute they were crying for him and his suffering, and the next minute angry that he would beat the crap out of his wife then go running to other women for comfort. But when he came on stage during a lovemaking scene without a shirt on, Dawn knew that she wanted to meet him after the show and Chena needed to make that happen. They met briefly since he was surrounded by fans and press.

It wasn't until the spring that they ran into each other at a Vertigo Sky Lounge. It was a relaxed setting, good music, wine, sexy cocktails, smoking cigars and weed on the patio outside. With a body of an Olympic athlete coupled with stilettos, Dawn was hard to miss in a crowd. She headed to the patio to light up her stash. After one puff he approached her. The smoke didn't seem to bother him. Dawn was delighted that he already passed the first two tests: following her, and not being bothered by her herbal habit. For an actor, Vine had the worst conversational skills. Dawn chalked it up to him being nervous, like most men that she encounters. But she found his bashful nature cute and innocent. They exchanged information, but she let Vine know that she wouldn't be calling or sending text messages. Vine accepted that challenge and had been a fixture in her life since.

Dawn was expecting him home any minute now and she had a special surprise for him. While he worked at a local café where all the local actors go to unwind, she hit the pavement on go-sees for modeling gigs during the day. At night, Dawn was a bartender at The W Hotel. It may not seem glamorous, but the tips were generous, and she was able to meet all types of celebrities. The stronger she made the drinks the more the cash flowed from their hands to her pocket. Receiving a hotel key card to an invite-only-party, night cap, conversation, or a line of coke or smoking some weed was the norm too.

Even though Dawn loved Vine - in fact even more than she had intended - sometimes she could not resist the temptation to indulge with other men. The white men in New York didn't care about the color of her caramel colored skin tone. It was actually like a magnet for them. Dawn always moisturized her glowing skin daily — well, it was sort of her job to do that as a model. She was a tall graham cracker dipped in honey and caramel. Being seen with a tall, black, lean, sexy woman was like the new in thing, at least on the east coast. Unless you lived on a certain side of town in Chicago, interracial dating was frowned upon in the black community. Chicago had segregated neighborhoods, still in the new millennium. But New York was a melting pot and Dawn could be as liberal as she wanted without judgment. Her naturally curly hair was big and bouncy, often likened to Tracee Ellis Ross's hair. White men seemed to love that look; always asking to touch it. They just wanted to have a good time just as much as she did. No commitment. She figured it was no harm since these men were well connected in the fashion, movie or theater industry.

Dawn was able to model in a Christian Dior fashion show in Manhattan last year thanks to a customer whom she served one night at the bar. Donald Sugerman was an older white haired gentleman but had much sex appeal and swagger. He drank Scotch neat and no chaser. He smelled like stale cigars and Polo cologne. He intrigued Dawn with his wicked smile and gray eyes that undressed her. This wasn't hard to do because she doesn't leave much to the imagination when she was working the bar. It really helped with tips when they saw cleavage or her long, toned legs.

After his second round of Scotch, they exchanged information and he told her about the fashion show. Apparently, Mr. Sugerman was some hot-shot investor that funded shoes for the models. He guaranteed Dawn that her legs would be on the catwalk if she showed up for the rehearsal the following day. Of course, she did just that.

Unfortunately, he was in town with his wife, but that did not stop him from coming backstage to congratulate Dawn. His presence caught her off guard when he approached. There were so many people backstage hustling and bustling around, it was as if Mr. Sugerman appeared out of thin air. She was attempting to change out of the Dior evening gown when she saw him approach. That powdered pink, silk gown felt like butter on her skin. It flowed and swayed with every movement she made as if she were commanding it to do so.

Mr. Sugerman embraced her, moved her hair that was covering her right ear to the side and whispered, "Beautiful job."

He found the zipper on the back of the dress and finished the task for her. The strap fell softly to right shoulder, partially revealing her B-cup breasts thanks to the low plunging neckline. Dawn was nervous but enticed. Her eyes darted around the room to see if anyone was paying close attention to what was happening. But backstage at a fashion show it was the usual mayhem. Lots of chatter, laughter, shoes being collected, dresses being thrown and gathered by the hired staff, hair pieces being removed, and lots of naked bodies moving about. Before she had time to decide to have a conscience, Mr. Sugerman's hands found the opening slit in the front of the dress and stuck his finger deep inside of her. She gasped and he quickly covered her mouth with his to stifle her moans as he rapidly slid his finger in and out of her.

The way he had her pinned against the wall, his body pressed close to hers, it looked as if he was just kissing her. He pressed his thumb hard against her clitoris. Her knees buckled slightly and she was totally embarrassed. As he massaged her right breast that was now fully exposed, he sucked his middle finger cleaning it of all her moist evidence.

"You are a delicious pansy," he purred with a wicked grin. Mr. Sugerman promised that she would hear from him again and that they would "indulge fully in ecstasy". Dawn chuckled. Why couldn't he just say that they would fuck? She had not heard from him since that evening last year. He got his kicks and she got recognition. It was an even exchange as far as Dawn was concerned.

The battle of the sexes would cease if women only knew how to shut up, fuck them good, be arm candy, and bake them something special every once in a while, according to Dawn. That's how she dealt with Vine. She did not question him, and in return, he voluntarily gave information and updates about his life. She cooked the basic minimum, chicken breast, veggies, potatoes, very basic and he was grateful that she cooks at all. Then she would blow his mind with a feast with baked goodies and he thinks that she is the best thing that ever happened to him. Dawn dished out the sex sparingly, in the beginning, then after a couple of months, he was begging for mercy because she was wearing him out every chance that I had. In the shower, back of his car, during sports half-time, at the club in the men's bathroom, as soon as he walked through the door from work, even after they argued. Then she wouldn't let him touch her for another two weeks or more. It was a recipe that Dawn used for a few years on several men, and it worked every time.

She scurried to straighten the comforter on the bed as she heard Vine unlock the front door. Her mother's voice rang through her head each time she found herself being lazy. "No man wants to come home to a dirty, filthy house!" Dawn kept a very tidy apartment, but she didn't want to see any disappointment in Vine's face if he knew she lounged around all day. Vine believed in productivity whether it was of the mind or body. If he wasn't at the gym he was reading or meditating. He believed that there was always room for improvement in each day. Being idle was a pet peeve of his.

"Hey, babe," Vined said loud enough for Dawn to hear. As he tossed his keys on the counter Dawn appeared in the doorway with a smile and open arms. They embraced and kissed as if they had not seen each other in days.

"How was work?" Dawn asked.

"Pretty awesome today, actually," Vine replied. He opened the refrigerator and grabbed his Voss water bottle.

"Is that right," Dawn said and settled on a bar stool. Here she was ready to tell him some news, but he had some for her. Since he began first, she decided to share her news later.

"It was an ordinary day until I made a specialty Espresso con Panna for a customer who turned out to be a producer for Tyler Perry." Vine gulped his water down with a smile on his face.

Dawn hated when he bragged about his coffee making skills. She had no interest in coffee at all and he knew it. If she ever needed a jolt a line of coke did a way better job than any coffee ever could, but she never told him that. Vine liked to mention coffee just to get underneath her skin and it worked every time until now.

"Wait! Are you serious?" Dawn clasped her hands together and mashed them against her lips. This could be the moment they both had been waiting for in his career.

"Yep!" His smile grew wider. "You know I handed him my headshot from my stash behind the counter, right?"

"See? I told you that would come in handy!"

"You did, babe, and you were right!" Vine winked at her. "Well, he said that I would be a great fit for a recurring role on the new season of 'The Haves and Have Nots'."

Dawn's mouth flew open and tears formed in her eyes. She was genuinely happy for his moment. Vine walked towards her, turning the stool around so that she was facing him. He stood between her legs and stared at her lovingly.

"The only thing is filming begins next month in Atlanta, but the company is going to Chicago around the same time."

"That's a no-brainer, Vine. To hell with *Stomp*! This is your opportunity for your face to be seen, your voice to heard, your acting career is about to take off!"

"I knew you would say that," he kissed her forehead. "But you know my heart is for the stage."

"Vine Clarke! Are we really having this conversation right now?" Dawn wanted to slap him into reality. She wanted to remind him that he had not stepped foot on a stage since he joined the company for *Stomp* but thought better of it. "You're an actor, whether on stage or on screen. The screen is calling you. The universe is pushing you into another direction. What did you tell the man?"

"I'm going for a screen test tomorrow," he laughed and walked away. "You know I had to mess with you a little bit. It's good to see you're on my side, babe."

Dawn looked around for something to throw at him, but by that time he was already in the bedroom. "Don't play with my heart like that, boy!" She followed him in the bedroom and hopped on the bed. "I'm so happy for you, babe. We've been waiting for this moment for so long.

You were in the right place at the right time." She helped him finish taking off his shirt, ran her fingers down his chest and across his abs.

"You got that right. The timing is perfect," Vine said and stroked the side of her face. "And he even liked his coffee." Vine smirked a little. He was clearly pleased with himself.

Dawn pulled him in and kissed his belly button and his hip bones while she unbuttoned his slacks. Vine played in her hair mindlessly. He was more focused on the erection that was rising simply from her touch.

"Oh, before you get carried away down there," Vine said, lifting Dawn's chin up. "I got your text earlier. What did you want to share with me?"

"It can wait, babe," Dawn replied, smiling. Her surprise announcement could definitely wait for now. It was nothing in comparison to this news.

"You sure?"

"I'm so proud of you. Now let me show you how much," she said, pulling down his boxers. She held a firm grip on his erect manhood and slipped him into her mouth.

Vine rubbed her hair softly and moaned.

"Thank you, babe."

4

Jonetta

Jonetta felt the blood drain from her face and her hands became dank with sweat. She could not believe her eyes. What was *he* doing here? She had not seen him since that God-awful night. Her emotions flooded her thoughts almost paralyzing her movement. Jonetta inhaled and reminded herself that she was no longer a naïve twenty-some-thing- year-old, but rather an almost sixty-year-old woman with grown children. What if one of her daughters were there visiting? She winced at the thought of them knowing who he was and what type of low-life world he actually came from. She would either have to explain who he was or rather come up with an incredible lie. Neither of which she was ever prepared to do because she thought her past was buried. It never occurred to her that any of it would resurface, especially not this late in life. Her daughters and her ex-husband, Norman, could never know the truth about her past. But here it was, her past, on her doorstep. He had a lot of nerve showing up unannounced. Now she was growing angry.

Jonetta finally got her thoughts in order and snatched the door open, "What are you doing here?" She demanded in the nastiest tone she could muster.

He grinned flashing his gold-capped tooth that he must have gotten later on in life. Jonetta was sure that she would have remembered that hideous thing otherwise.

"Well, hello to you too Johnnie. May I?" He asked and removed his charcoal gray fedora which revealed his silky gray hair that was apparently holding on to his scalp for dear life.

Jonetta stepped aside to allow him to enter her house. She checked the streets to see if anyone had noticed his presence. It was a brisk, autumn afternoon and only a few kids were at play. She was safe with her secrets so far. Swiftly, she closed the door behind him.

"Nobody calls me that anymore," she retorted. "And you didn't answer my question." Jonetta pulled a cigarette from her pack of Marlboros. Big Louie pulled a lighter from his pocket and lit her cigarette. She motioned for him to have a seat on the olive green, velour sofa as she sat in a matching chair.

He huffed when he sat down and spread his legs really wide and grinned. "I will admit, this is not a social visit," he replied with the same thick Haitian accent that used to make the hair on the back of her neck rise and give her a wicked chill. But now she was simply annoyed by his foreign dialect.

Jonetta was much older now and grew much thicker skin over the years. There was not much of anything that intimidated her anymore until now.

"I'll get straight to it. Mr. Lucky had a debt to pay, and since he left everything to you, the way I see it, it's now your debt to pay."

"His debt was buried with him along with the rest of his secrets and private affairs," Jonetta pulled a drag on her Marlboro casually. She took her time blowing out the smoke and continued, "Besides, he's been dead well damn near forty years, why are you coming around here trying to cause trouble now?"

"I've been a little... incapacitated, but that's neither here nor there. A debt is a debt," Big Louie pulled at his lapels and stuck his chest out. "I'm here to collect."

"I think you mean *incarcerated*," Jonetta said, blowing out another thick cloud of smoke. She had heard some years back that he was thrown in jail for drug smuggling and human trafficking young Haitian girls. He must have had some sharp, high priced lawyer because with those felony charges he should have been locked up for life.

Big Louie was not impressed. He sucked on a toothpick as he eyed her from head to toe. "I'm back in town for good, Johnnie. It's sort of a new beginning for me. I'm a minister now down at the First Temple of God."

"Hell must have frozen over and somebody forgot to tell me," Jonetta sneered. "You've always been the leader of a pack, but this time, you've taken it to a new level, huh? Don't tell me, the ladies' usher board is your new harem and the deacons are the pimps."

"I'll tell you what," Big Louie said and stood up as if he was preparing to make a great offer. "Why don't you come down and visit one Sunday. See for yourself that I'm a changed man. But either way, I'll be back in two weeks. That's enough time for you to pray on it or come to your senses."

Jonetta shrugged. "You can come back tomorrow and the next day for all I care, my answer will still be the same. I'm not responsible for paying a forty-year-old debt that had nothing to do with me in the first place!"

Big Louie eyed the living room and sneered, "You know, I recall this house looking much better than this. Seems to me at your age you really don't need all of this space. It's more a burden on you than a blessing, right?" He nodded as if he had answered his own question. "This house would actually cover the debt. I could renovate it and make this my kingdom quite nicely." He scanned the house as far as his eyes could see and nodded in agreement with himself.

"What type of debt did Mr. Lucky owe you exactly?"

"The type of debt that a house like this would actually cover."

Jonetta raised one eyebrow only the way she could that warned people to tread lightly and choose their next words carefully. She put out her cigarette with force in a metal ashtray with her eyes still locked with his.

"So now you think that you can bully me from my home? I earned everything that I acquired. No two-bit-washed up-hustler-played-out-pimp-wanna-be-preacher is going to rob me of it. Not in this lifetime!"

Big Louie stepped closer to her so that he was now standing over her where she sat. Jonetta rose to the occasion and now his belly was almost touching her breasts. She could smell the stench of his strong, bitter cologne and stale cigar breath. But she stood her ground and continued to hold his stare.

"You got a lot of mouth on you for a tiny woman," he said and placed his fedora on top of his balding head. Jonetta was petite and only stood five feet four inches, but she had heart. "Like I said, I'll be back."

"New levels, new devils," Jonetta countered with hands on her hips. "Come back if you dare. However, I can't guarantee the visit will such as nice as this one."

"I'll see myself out. Have a good day, Johnnie," Big Louie said and slammed the front door.

Jonetta was furious that he had the nerve to show up unannounced demanding that she pay a debt that her pimp and lover owed two decades ago. True, the house was falling apart over the years and she had been considering moving in with Georgia anyway, but she was not about to be forced out, and especially not by the likes of Big Louie.

Jonetta walked to the kitchen to pour a glass Scotch that she had on reserve for only special occasions. Her nerves were rattled and her hands shook as she gulped down the alcohol. She turned on the faucet for cold water and splashed some on her face. If Jonetta's children only knew exactly what she did with men regularly before their father came along they would probably lose all respect for her. She would never give them the satisfaction of knowing her past. Everyone from her shameful past, she thought, was dead and gone from Chicago. Jonetta never worried about her secret being exposed until now.

Hunched over the sink, while allowing the droplets of water splatter in the sink, she allowed her mind to roll back in time. Jonetta recalled the first time she met Big Louie in that very house for his birthday party. A night she could never forget.

Jonetta had just finished making love to Mr. Lucky when the guests arrived an hour later. There were only a few people, mostly couples except the birthday boy, Big Louie. He had a thick accent and rich cocoa skin. His eyes were wide as was his nose. His hair was mildly seasoned with salt and pepper with deep waves and slicked back. He had a huge belly that was solid. It didn't jiggle when he laughed at all. It just stuck out there wanting to be seen. He kept staring at Jonetta all night and winked at her from across the room a couple of times. She pretended not to see and avoided conversation with him. Mr. Lucky walked her directly over to him at one point for an introduction, "This is my friend, Big Louie. We go way back. He's from Haiti. I remember when he first got to Chicago, I had to take him under my wing," Mr. Lucky boasted, but Big Louie scoffed and puffed his cigar. "Don't be shy, baby. He won't bite." He left it at that and didn't bother with the details on just how they knew each other.

He was successful as a restaurant owner in Chicago. "People love strange food. No matter how it tastes. They love trying something new, yes?"

Jonetta smiled and nodded politely. They were interrupted by somebody playing a record by The Miracles. The ladies screamed and paired up with their men to dance.

"C'mon, dance for us baby," Mr. Lucky said and kissed Jonetta's neck down to her breast. She squealed with delight and protested from embarrassment. "Oh, don't mind Big Louie. He certainly don't mind us."

Jonetta obliged and began slow dancing to "Ooo Baby Baby", by the Miracles, for Mr. Lucky and Big Louie since he was looking with greedy eyes.

Mr. Lucky grunted and nudged Big Louie. "Look at those hips!"

After a few more songs were played the guests began to leave. They thanked Mr. Lucky for a good time as always. Then it was just down to Mr. Lucky, Big Louie, and Jonetta. She wished the birthday boy would disappear too so they could be alone again. But apparently he was staying the evening as Mr. Lucky told her later on. They sat down and talked about the difference in music on the islands and in Africa than the Americanized Negro music.

"I forgot my smokes in the room, I'll be back," Mr. Lucky announced.

"I'll get them," Jonetta offered as an escape from Big Louie's gaze.

"Sit tight, baby, I said I'll get them. Keep the birthday boy company." He winked at her and disappeared into the back room.

Jonetta looked longingly after him as he disappeared down the hall.

"Don't worry, he'll be back." Big Louie laughed. He got up to dance with her quickly grabbing her around the waist. He puffed his cigar and blew smoke in the air. Jonetta found a reason to escape his grasp by coughing, but just as she almost left his reach, he snatched her back to him lifting her off of her feet and twirling her around. Her eyes got big and his gleamed with pleasure.

"You like my style?" He asked placing her back on her feet. He put out his cigar and placed it in the ashtray. "Come here, sweet lady," he said grabbing her wrist. "Let me show you my other moves." Jonetta obliged him reluctantly. She glanced back and forth down the hall wishing Mr. Lucky would return, but he didn't. Big Louie pressed his manhood against her and asked, "Do you feel that? That's for you, baby." He lunged in to kiss her but she pulled back.

"No," she said pushing his chest. "Lucky will be back soon. You don't want to upset him, do you?"

"Upset him? Why would it upset him when he gave you to me for my birthday present?"

Before Jonetta could let his last remark sink in her head, his hand was already up her dress snatching her panties down. She fought him off, but he was strong. Big Louie hoisted her up in one arm and carried her to the plush, velvet sofa and threw her down like a rag doll. He grunted and licked his lips while he unbuckled his belt.

"Turn around," he ordered.

Jonetta shook her head no and whimpered. He proceeded to whip her with the belt. Jonetta yelped, but he demanded that she keep her mouth shut. "You think you special?" he demanded grabbing her hair at the nape of her neck. "You're not! You're just a whore like the others he keeps. Now turn around and bend over." She did as she was told because from the look in his eyes she knew he meant business. He showed her just how average she was as he forced himself into her flesh. Jonetta had been raped before so she allowed herself to mentally escape while he thrust himself inside of her like he was angry. He held on tight to her hips to make sure she felt every inch of him. Jonetta thought it would never end. She felt her insides getting raw and dry with each thrust. When he finished, he kept himself inside of her trying to catch his breath.

"You like that? I'm better than Lucky, huh?" He pulled himself out and snatched her by her hair. "I asked you a question, girl."

"Yes," she nodded and whimpered.

"Good. I'll want more later on," he said and pulled a wad of bills out of his pocket. "This is for now," he waved a hundred dollar bill in her face and stuffed into her bra. "This is for later," he said and placed another hundred on the coffee table.

Jonetta curled up into a ball on the sofa and exhaled as he left the living room. Where did Mr. Lucky go? As a few more moments passed, she heard him approaching the living room. She sat up straight as if she were the one in trouble for doing something wrong. She shook her head and began to weep.

"What are you crying for, Johnnie? Did he hurt you?" Mr. Lucky caressed her face, carefully examining it.

She whimpered. "He forced himself on me, whipped me like I was a damn child and grabbed my hair! I didn't want to do it. He made me do it."

"You were his birthday gift from me to him," Mr. Lucky announced as if she knew that this was the plan all along. "Johnnie, if you felt like you were treated like a child, maybe it's because you were behaving like a child like you're doing now," Mr. Lucky said folding his arms across his chest and raised his eyebrows. "I thought you were a woman."

"No, I was not behaving like a child," Jonetta protested, standing to her feet to defend herself. "I am a woman. But I thought you loved me as *your* woman. Where did you go? How could you just offer me up like you don't give a damn about me? And what other women do you have?"

Mr. Lucky shook his head and disregarded those questions because he couldn't believe just how naive she was. Instead, he got straight down to business. "How much did he pay you?" Jonetta reached into her bra and showed him the hundred dollar bill and pointed to the table. He snatched the bill from her and replied, "This is mine for now, and that's yours when you earn it." He said pointing to the bill on the table.

Jonetta was appalled and saddened by his behavior. She didn't understand how a man who just made such passionate love to her could offer her to his friend as a "birthday gift" in the same night. She bit her lip and tried not to cry. Mr. Lucky held her close and lifted her chin, "Come here, baby. Don't cry. You did good. You must've really done well pleasing him for him to leave money on the table like that." He kissed her and stroked the back of her head. He slipped his hand between her legs and pushed her away quickly. "What the hell is this?" He asked lifting up his moist fingers. "You didn't make him use protection? Are you trying to have his baby? The only baby you're gonna be having around here is mine! Didn't your aunts teach you anything?" He ranted pointing in her face not allowing her to answer. Jonetta didn't hear anything past the baby part.

"You want me to have your baby?" She was thrilled at the thought and it sounded as if he was jealous. She was pleased and confused all at the same time.

"We'll talk about that later," he said. "Look, I don't want you smelling like no other man when I'm ready for my turn!" He shook his head and caressed her shoulders and looked deep into her eyes. "He's back there resting. Go clean yourself up, lay down next to him and earn the rest of that money, and make him use protection this time, Johnnie."

Jonetta was confused. Hadn't she just suffered enough? Her insides were throbbing and it felt like she was on fire. Her eyes watered up, "You want me to go back there... with him? Why?"

"Baby, this is no different than what you do at your aunts' house. You're a prostitute and so are your aunts," he said not to be mean, but matter-of-fact. "I love them, just as I have come to love you. I won't let anything happen to you. When you're finished come lay with me."

That night she realized that the man she loved, Mr. Lucky, had just become her pimp. A piece of her became cold and numb. She was angry at herself for believing that a man could possibly love her for who she was instead of what she did to survive. Whenever Big Louie would come to "visit", Jonetta managed to remain out of sight because she feared that he would want another turn at being vicious and greedy with her body.

Anger festered inside of her, even up to this very moment, because she had not left Mr. Lucky sooner. She was weak back then. Dead inside. By the time she met Norman Miller, her ex-husband, she simply went through the motions of what she thought a wife should be to a man. The love she once craved didn't matter anymore. Then the children came along, three daughters. She poured whatever love she had left inside of her into them. And it wasn't much.

The phone rang. Jonetta shook her head, trying to clear the unwanted memories. It was her sister, Georgia.

Jonetta sighed.

After their Aunt Betty Lou's funeral, Jonetta located her older sister, Georgia, in New York and implored her to visit Chicago. It had become lonely and depressing not having any family in Chicago especially since her daughters had their own lives and barely called to check on her. Jonetta needed a connection to something or someone familiar and returning to Pennsylvania was out of the question. Georgia agreed to visit after all it had been decades since she laid eyes on her sister.

During her visit accompanied by her husband, Frederick Steinberg, they decided that Chicago was a perfect place to open another clothing boutique. The one in New York was flourishing and managed well in their absence. Since it would be easier for Fred to handle business matters, he stayed to rent out their aunts' home and begin preparation for their new boutique location while Georgia returned to New York to pack their belongings and have them sent to Chicago.

At the time, Jonetta was grateful to have a family member in the same city, and it resolved her issue of having two homes to maintain: the one that her aunts owned and the one she inherited from Mr. Lucky. She had stored most of their aunts' belongings in the basement until she could sort through it all properly, but left it up to Fred to decide what to do with the furniture. He, being the businessman that he was, claimed that family heirlooms should stay within the family for a lifetime. The resolution was simple, don't touch it.

All of that seemed like a good idea a few years ago, but now all Georgia did was get underneath her skin. Georgia especially boiled her blood when she mentioned that her ex-husband, Norman, being a good man. As if! He was nothing but a thorn in Jonetta's side then and now. Besides, his belly was too big for a petite woman like Jonetta. She would not dream of that man climbing on top of her. Not only did that bother her, but he now wore his silver hair slicked back into a ponytail. Jonetta didn't care how good Georgia thought he was, she perfectly fine alone.

Jonetta considered letting her go straight to voicemail. But she finally answered on the fourth ring.

"Hello?"

"Jonetta, you have to come quickly!" Georgia sobbed. "It's Fred. He had a heart attack!"

5

Colette

Colette stared at her baby girl as she nursed her and sighed. Delilah had to be the greediest baby of all of her children. Between Owen and the baby tugging on her breasts constantly they began to crack and bleed. The doctor warned it could cause serious infection to her and the baby, but Owen ignored her as usual until it couldn't be ignored anymore. The right nipple had healed up nicely over the past few days so Colette designated that one to her baby and the left was still healing. She began to feel like a dairy cow and wasn't too far off from looking like one. The only thing she liked about her new body was her butt. It was much bigger and she knew her husband loved big butts.

But that did not attract Owen as much as she had hoped. He had not touched her in a while especially since he couldn't have his snack regularly anymore and he was staying out later than usual. When Colette mentioned it to him, the only response she got was his thick hand around her neck and more late nights. She didn't blame herself for that attack like she usually would though. Any wife with a brain would question her husband's unusual whereabouts, but Owen acted like he was above that. Colette was getting sick of his ways. She couldn't pray it away. She had to face it for who Owen was and how his behavior was affecting her and their children.

The older kids were asking for him at night and Colette had run out of excuses for his absence. She began to get frustrated dealing with the children alone. It was clear that Owen didn't care for her anymore, but at the very least he could have shown concern for their children, but he didn't even do that much. As much as she hated to admit it, her mother was right; she should not have gotten involved with the Aldridge family. They were known to be nothing but trouble makers and rough neck boys. But Colette was in love with Owen and he made her body feel so good. That was all in the past and now she had more than enough problems on her hands.

Her baby was done feeding and needed burping. This had become her life. She was miserable. After she swaddled Delilah and laid her back in the crib she decided to call Phyllis. Her government issued mobile phone was turned back on, thanks to her mother.

"Hey, sis," Colette tried to sound cheerful.

"What's up?" Phyllis answered dryly.

"Nothing much. You're home and I'm home, so I was just calling."

"Oh," Phyllis responded flatly. "Well, you know the only thing I'm doing is packing these days."

"Yeah, how's that coming along?" Colette asked trying to spark conversation.

"It's packing, Colette. Putting things in boxes, sealing them and repeat, ya know? Nothing exciting."

"Well, if you need to take a break you should come visit me and the baby," Colette offered. She was desperate for company. She certainly didn't expect her mother to return any time soon after their last visit. Colette was certain that she pissed her mother off because she had not heard from her since.

"I can't take a break. I'm packing a house, not a three bedroom apartment. Or is it a two bedroom apartment that you have?"

"Why do you have to be so nasty with me? I was just looking for conversation. It's not like I'm having fun either burping, nursing and changing dirty diapers all day either. Then dealing with the kids when they come with homework and cooking them dinner, worrying about Owen and repeat!"

"Well, you chose that life, girl," Phyllis remarked. "Where's your loser husband these days anyway?"

"Last I checked the same place as yours!"

"Excuse me?"

"He's at work, Phyllis. Or is Damien not working?"

"Don't be a smart ass and don't even try me. My man keeps a job, unlike yours."

"You can dish it, but you can't take it, as usual," Colette laughed. "Owen has been with Streets and Sanitation for ten years, what are you talking about?"

"And suspended from his job how many times? All he has to do is collect garbage and keep his nose clean. But he can't even do that! Look, I gotta get back to packing and watching this mess on television."

"What mess? Your reality shows?"

"No, smart ass. I'm watching the marches and protests happening all over the country for the injustice and brutality done to these un-armed black men by white cops. Have you been living under a rock or something? It's on regular television, you don't need cable to keep up with that news. Turn your T.V. on and you'll see. I swear it's like we've stepped back into the sixties."

Colette would have loved to turn on the television to watch the news coverage except she couldn't because in a fit of rage last week Owen threw his beer bottle at the television shattering the screen.

"I'll catch it some other time. Besides, I called to talk to you."

Phyllis sighed. "Didn't I just tell you that I have to finish packing?"

"You have a wireless Bluetooth, use it!" Colette insisted. Usually she would let her sister get off the phone, but she really needed to talk.

Phyllis sucked her teeth. "Hold on." Colette heard the connection to the Bluetooth and was surprised Phyllis actually did it. "Okay, I'm listening. Now what is so important?"

"I think that I'm going through post-partum depression," Colette confided in her sister. "I can't seem to get out of this funk that I'm feeling. All I do is take care of kids. Although, Delilah is a good baby, I'm just sick of this. I need a break. The first time I put on real clothes was when I took her to the six week checkup appointment. My boobs hurt from this milk that I've been carrying around for two years. Owen only has sex with me from the back. I know I've gained weight, but..."

"Okay...What do you want me to say to that?" Phyllis quipped. "You are not the first woman to suffer from post-partum depression and you won't be the last. Find something to do with yourself other than be a mom twenty-four-seven. Anybody would go nuts living the way you do. Once Delilah gets older, go back to school, take an art class, or go to a mommy-and-me class with her now so you can meet other women. Having friends or a network of people going through the same thing always helps. Mama said you got your tubes tied, thank God, so try doing something with your life."

"All of that requires money," Colette sighed. "Thanks for the pep-talk, but I thought that you could be part of my network of friends, but as a sister, because you're a housewife, just like me."

"Look, I don't know what to tell you. I'm sure you qualify for financial aid since you already get the Link card. We all have problems. We have to move and the holidays are right around the corner. This is awful timing. We also have to uproot the girls and send them to a different school because we basically suck at budgeting. But I'm going to ensure that this never happens again! What are you going to do to ensure a new life for yourself?"

"Wait. Damien wasn't paying the rent?" Colette inquired. It was the first she heard about that.

"Never mind about all of that!" Phyllis snapped. "You totally missed the point."

"I got your point. I'll figure out what to do with myself eventually. I just didn't know that's the reason you were moving."

"Everybody knows that except you, so don't go running back to mama like you always do with some newsflash. She knows. Okay?"

Phyllis always maintained since they were kids that Colette was a chronic tattle tell.

Colette ignored her sister's snide comment and continued, "But if you're not working, just like me, and Damien is making all the money, just like Owen, then where is the money going if it's not to the rent?"

"Why are you always comparing yourself to me?" Phyllis demanded. "We're nothing alike. And furthermore, didn't I just say don't worry about all of that? I got this!"

"God, sometimes I wish that mama would've swallowed you instead!" Colette said and ended the call. "What a bitch!"

Phyllis had a lot of nerve pretending that she was any better than Colette because the only difference between them was minus two kids and a couple of pounds. Colette got some satisfaction from knowing that her sister really wasn't any better off than she was. She figured that Damien probably was spending his money on another woman or family somewhere for that matter. But who would blame him? Phyllis was such a bitch by nature and never even tried to hide it. Colette wouldn't be surprised if he had another kid somewhere as desperately as he wanted one all those years Phyllis struggled to get pregnant. Colette grinned at the thought during those four months Damien refused to "do his job" with Phyllis that he probably stepped out on her. Like her mother always told them, men can't go that long without a good release.

Owen had not bothered to touch her since he won the two-hundred dollars that day. She knew that he was probably cheating with the same bitch she caught him with last year. "Shante from around the way" as everyone who grew up with her referred to her. Everyone knew about them sneaking around and it embarrassed Colette to the point where she tried to fight her while she was pregnant with Delilah. Shante could have any man she wanted because she was beautiful and successful as a realtor. Colette knew that Shante only wanted Owen for one reason because he certainly didn't have anything else to offer but good dick.

Speak of the devil, Colette heard him coming through the door. She glanced at the clock. What the hell was he doing home at one o'clock in the afternoon?

"Well, hello," Colette greeted him with her arms folded across her chest.

"Hey," he said and walked right past her avoiding eye contact.

"Don't tell me, you lost your job," she huffed.

"Okay," he shrugged. "I won't tell you then." Owen headed to the kitchen for a beer and slammed the refrigerator door when he didn't see one. "Where the hell are my beers?"

"You drank them all and threw one at the television," she responded casually.

He walked up to her snarling, but Colette stood her ground. Owen pointed his finger at her a couple of times and walked away. "You know what? Your mouth is only good for one thing, and it ain't talking!"

Colette's mouth flew open. She couldn't believe that her husband had just disrespected her in that manner.

"Yeah, keep it open just like that! I got something to put in it." He grabbed his crotch for emphasis.

"Get away from me!" Colette shooed him away. "You are so foul!"

"Come here," he grabbed her arm and pulled her close to him. Colette struggled to release herself from his tight hold. "A man can't get no beer when he comes home, can't get no head, can't get no peace!" He shoved her on the sofa and stood over her. "The least you can do is make me feel good when I come home. But that's okay, you give lazy head anyway." Owen walked away laughing.

"Look who's talking!"

Owen turned around quickly. "You know what? I'm so sick of you! I'm sick of these kids. I'm sick of this cramped apartment. I'm just sick and tired of living like this with your fat ass!"

"Well that makes two of us!"

"Oh yeah?" Owen walked up to her again. "You know the difference though?"

"What's that?" Colette quipped and folded her arms across her chest.

"I'm actually gonna do something about it!"

"Like what?"

"Like leave!" Owen yelled in her face.

Colette swallowed hard, and blinked her eyes repeatedly trying to bite back tears. It would not be the first time he left, but he always came back. Still the thought of him leaving her with four kids alone fright-ened her this time.

"Well, it wouldn't be the first time, Owen. What's stopping you this time?" She tried to save face best she could. She swung open her arms waiting for an answer.

"You ain't said nothing but a word." Owen nodded his head, pacing back and forth. "I knew the day would come you would think that you're better off without me. Soon as I don't bring home enough money or lay the pipe for you, I'm no good for you anymore, huh? The government is your new man anyway, right?"

"What are you talking about?" Colette huffed. "Are you high right now? You must be on that stuff again, because that's always been our situation and I'm still here encouraging you, cooking for you, having your babies and raising them. All the while the only thing you give me is black eyes and a broken heart."

He chuckled to himself for a moment like only an asshole would. "Yeah, I'm high right now and so what?" He folded his arms across his chest. "I haven't given you a black eye in years, so stop it! And who cares if your heart is broken, huh? I sure as hell don't!"

"Clearly, you don't care about me or your kids. So, how soon can you leave?"

"I care about my kids, but don't even think about hitting me with child support!" Owen warned. "I have a good woman who takes care of me and she makes me feel like a king. Shante buys me nice clothes, takes me to nice restaurants, and she even bought me a new car for all of the hard work I do for her on the houses she owns and in the bedroom." He grabbed his crotch again.

"Shante? You stupid son-of-a-bitch! She's just using you and as soon as she's done you'll be crawling back to me, but I'm not taking you back this time! IT. IS. OVER!" Colette ran to their bedroom and began toss-ing dresser drawers and snatching his clothes out of the closet. "Here! Come get your shit! Take all of it and never come back!"

Owen came around the corner and shook his head. "I don't need none of that shit, girl. I didn't come home early to pack. I came here to say good-bye to your tired, fat ass. Look at you. Just pathetic. You used to be so damn fine that all the men wanted you! I was proud to have you on my arm. Now you let yourself go having all of these kids. You're lucky that I still want to even fuck you. How much longer did you think I was going to stick around?" He looked around the room in disgust.

"I'm going to kill you!" Colette screamed and ran across the room but tripped on the corner of the bed landing on the floor in front of Owen. She winced and grabbed her hip bone rolling to her side.

Owen chuckled.

"That's what you get! Get your ass up!" Owen demanded. But Colette continued to lie on the floor, she was embarrassed and in pain. He helped her up to her feet then pushed her on the bed. "Sit your ass down! What did you think that you were about to do?"

He wrapped his thick, rough hand around her neck. Colette shivered with fear. He was strong enough to snap her neck if he applied enough pressure. "You're so pathetic. But, hey, look at it this way, now you can get more government assistance now that I'm gone, right?" His eyes glowered.

Colette's eyes were bulging and turning red so he released his hold and pushed her back on the bed. She gasped for air and coughed.

"Get out! You're high as a kite! Just get out!" Colette screamed. She was actually afraid of what he would do next.

He climbed on top of her, held her hands above her head and got close to her face as possible.

"Get off of me!" She cried.

"You know that I love you. I don't love her ass. I've always loved *you*, but I was never good enough. Just another fucked up Aldridge boy fucking up a good girl's life, right?" Owen let her hands go, but stayed straddled on top of her.

Colette lied stiff as she released hot tears. She swallowed hard as her heart raced. Usually his emotions were all over the place when he dabbled in cocaine. She was unsure what to expect next from him.

"Did you ever really love me?" Owen asked if he desperately wanted an answer.

"Yes!" Colette cried out. "Of course I love you!"

But that response seemed to anger Owen instead. "Turn your lying ass over!" He flipped her onto her stomach and raised her house dress. She heard him unbuckle his pants, and then unzip them.

Colette whimpered. She knew exactly what was coming next. It was his new form of punishment for her, one that he actually enjoyed.

"No! Owen, please," she pleaded. "I'm sorry!"

Owen smacked the sides of her large butt and a loud cracking sound ripped through the air.

Colette whimpered.

"Please, what?" He smacked her again harder.

Colette cried out that time.

"You're sorry, huh?" Again, he smacked her as hard as he could.

Colette screamed from the pain from his thick hand.

"Too late!"

He spread her cheeks and spit. She felt the glob land right where he was about to enter. Before she could protest again, it was too late, just like he said. Owen had inserted himself inside of Colette as rough as he could. He moaned and grunted loudly.

Colette buried her face into the mattress to smother her cries. The last thing she wanted was anyone calling the police because she knew it would be over soon. This had been Owen's substitute for her black eyes and split lips. Entering the smallest, tightest hole on her body forcefully excited him. It made him feel powerful and in control.

Owen would go for months of not touching her at all to sucking her breasts full of milk whenever he chose, choking and punching her, having sex too soon after each baby, to rough anal sex. It was all his way of showing Colette that her body belonged to him. Period.

Before, her busted lips made it almost impossible to even talk after a fight with Owen, and now she could barely walk afterwards. But if Colette had to choose her form of physical abuse, it would be rough anal sex. Although it was painful every time at least nobody could physically see this type of abuse on her body; save for her gynecologist who warned her that it could cause permanent damage. But she reasoned that it was better than black eyes.

From the outside looking in, though, it appeared that Owen had finally stopped physically abusing Colette, but they both knew better. Owen grabbed her shoulders, and huffed with each pump. Colette held on tight to the blanket gripping through the pain. He counted out loud as he thrust himself deeper inside of her. After seventeen pumps, his highest count yet, he was finally finished. He grunted, beat his chest like wild man and collapsed on top of her breathing heavily. Colette tried to catch her breath as she sobbed. This time was too rough and painful. She knew he meant to hurt her badly and he succeeded.

"Shante, uppity ass, won't let me do this to her." He admitted breathing heavily, patting Colette on the head. "I'm really going to miss this tight ass right here, babe. Almost made it to twenty pumps this time," he said proudly. Owen pumped one more time for emphasis' sake. Finally, he snatched himself out of Colette then wiped himself off with their blanket. Colette, still stiff, was in disbelief, ashamed and disgusted.

"Baby, I'm actually doing you a favor by leaving," he announced as he tucked in his shirt and fastened his pants. "Be sure to tell your mama that much, too. Oh, yeah, I'll call when I want to see my kids and when I want some of that ass. We're still married so you can't keep my kids or that ass from me. I still got papers on you. Remember that."

Colette gasped for air. "You can't leave!" she cried out. "I'm pregnant." Even after all of that, she was desperate and wanted Owen to see that leaving her was a big mistake especially now that she was expecting another child. His child. Their fifth child together.

Owen chuckled to himself.

"What else is new?"

He left the room and slammed the door on his way out. Delilah began to cry and Colette joined her.

6

Jonetta

Jonetta knew that Big Louie had threatened to return, but if he did she would not have known. After receiving the phone call from Georgia about Fred having a heart attack, Jonetta immediately rushed to the hospital and had not returned home but only a few times over the past few weeks to gather clothing and toiletries for herself.

Fred was in the intensive care unit and quite frankly it was not looking good for his recovery. He had an IV in his arm, heart monitor wires hanging from his chest and a tube down his throat. He only came to twice since he was admitted to the hospital. Georgia knew that a good outcome was not in his favor, but she never mentioned it aloud. She didn't have to because her body language said it all, especially when she placed her head at his feet.

Jonetta knew then that her sister was in no condition to think about anything but being by Fred's side. So she decided to stay with Georgia since her house was closer to the hospital anyway. She also offered to help around the house with anything that she needed, especially cooking. To make really good use of herself she also insisted that she check in on the staff at the store to let them know someone was still in charge, but Georgia reassured her that wouldn't be necessary. The last thing Georgia wanted was her sister bullying her employees.

Jonetta wasn't necessarily pleased to be back in the house that held so many terrible memories, but Georgia and Fred repainted and rearranged furniture in such a way that it really didn't look like the same house on the inside. Nevertheless, the memories were still there. She busied herself by making stews and soups to freeze for Georgia. She could take them to the hospital with her or eat them whenever she decided to come home.

While getting much needed groceries for the house and her soup recipes, she had inquired casually to the cashier, Tracey, at the local grocery store about the "new minister" in the neighborhood. She always had the latest updates on neighborhood gossip. Tracey confirmed that Minister Louis Paul had a Homecoming service a few Sundays ago. She seemed impressed by him and the sermon he delivered about forgiveness and redemption. Jonetta scoffed, but maintained her composure.

"Minister Louis Paul? So that's his name?" Jonetta pondered aloud.

"Yes, do you know him?" Tracey asked anxiously.

"No," Jonetta lied. "It's just an interesting name, that's all."

"He's from Haiti. All of their names are backwards over there." Tracey offered information that Jonetta already knew. "He said that he lost family members in the earthquake there a few years ago. We've set up a relief fund, and the Outreach Committee is going to begin collecting canned goods and shoes for the people."

Now that was information Jonetta didn't know about, but found interesting. But she really wanted so badly to tell this poor girl that she was sure the money was going to be used on whatever he pleased and that the Red Cross and their government were already handling those relief efforts. But she left it alone because some people will follow a man straight into the ocean if he claimed he saw Jesus there. According to Jonetta, church members were a bunch of broke fools looking to a man to be saved. She figured that's why the majority of the congregation was women. If they just took the time to see how well their ministers lived compared to how they lived they would smarten up. But that was none of her concern.

Tracey continued her babbling and Jonetta hated that she even asked until she mentioned something about a house. "Minister Paul also mentioned buying a new house in the Pill Hill neighborhood, not too far from here..."

Buying? Jonetta snatched her dollar bills from the cashier's hand, at that news, picked up her grocery bags and dropped them in her cart so abruptly that it caused other shoppers to stop and stare. Once she realized that she was causing a scene she flashed a smiled and said, "Have a good one, I have to get going."

She made a mental to note to find out about Minister Louis' other efforts. What other lies was he telling people? Jonetta knew full well that his intentions were not to buy her house, but rather take it from her. Take from her what was rightfully given and earned. All the years of hard work, dedication, and giving of her mind, body, and soul that she did for Mr. Lucky felt justified when he left the house, minks, and jewelry to her in his will. It couldn't erase painful memories, but at least she had something to show for it.

Although Jonetta felt sorry for Fred's condition she did see this situation as an opportunity to make a clean break without anyone being suspicious. The last thing she wanted to do was give in to Big Louie's "suggestion" about giving him the house. She hated being defeated, it made her cringe, but it seemed reasonable. Jonetta rarely gave God the credit for anything, but this couldn't be anything but God. Needing to take care of Georgia's affairs and the house would be her cover to finally leave behind her past once and for all. It was a blessing in disguise indeed. She knew her daughters would ask plenty of questions, but this was a logical explanation.

As she put away the groceries one thought after the other raced through her mind about her next plan of action. Her smartphone rang, and without looking for it in the bottom of her purse she knew it was Colette's ring tone. Jonetta sighed because she was not in the mood to talk to her daughter, but decided to answer it.

"Hello."

"Hi mama," Colette sighed. "Are you busy?"

"Always, but I answered the phone."

Colette began to sob, but gathered herself to continue. "Owen left us. We had a big argument and he left to be with Shante."

"What?" Jonetta exclaimed. She put the package of chicken quarters in the refrigerator and sat down at Georgia's nicely decorated kitchen table. "When did this happen and who is Shante?"

"Mama, you know, the same trifling trick that he was cheating on me with when I was pregnant with Delilah. Well, he moved in with her! He came home yesterday in the middle of the afternoon and just made an announcement and left."

"Niggas and flies, I do despise," Jonetta retorted.

"Mama, please," Colette pleaded.

"Well, sounds like he never stopped cheating on you with her," Jonetta retorted. "He didn't just decide this out the blue, ya know? But never mind that damn fool! Did he hit you?"

"No."

"Colette," Jonetta probed.

"I swear, he didn't, mama," Colette said.

"Well, good riddance to him then," Jonetta said. She reached for her pack of cigarettes and lit one. "When something is lost, something better is gained."

"He's not lost. I know exactly where to find my husband!" Colette fumed. "Mama, what am I supposed to do?"

"Live, survive, and move on," Jonetta replied. "That's what women do. We survive and move on with our lives. Since you never saved a dime like I repeatedly told you to do, you'll have to rely upon government assistance. You really can't expect a man like Owen to rightfully take care of his children so make sure you file for a divorce as soon as you can so it can be on file for child support. I'm sure he took the car, so you'll have to get used to riding public transportation..."

"He told me not to even think about filing for child support," Colette cried, interrupting her mother's check list for ending a marriage.

"What? He's reached an all-time low!" Jonetta exclaimed. "Don't let me catch that low life on the street!"

"I just can't believe this is happening," Colette sobbed. "What am I supposed to tell the kids? They don't even know yet."

"Well, where the hell do they think their father is exactly?"

"I told them he had to work late," Colette sighed. "I didn't know what else to say. I'm not like Phyllis. I can't just come up with quick lies on the spot."

Jonetta shook her head and took another puff of her cigarette. She blew a cloud of smoke up towards the ceiling and nodded. Colette was right about that, she was nothing like Phyllis when it came to thinking on her feet. Even when she was a young girl Jonetta always knew when Colette was lying because she was fidgety and the tone of her voice would fluctuate. Phyllis on the other hand would tell a stone faced lie and have everyone believing it.

But Jonetta always knew that Colette would make poor choices as a grown woman because she made stupid ones as a child. Like the time when she was in third grade, a jealous classmate cut Colette's ponytail off with a pair of scissors. Colette claimed that she snatched the scissors away from her, but returned them to her because she didn't want to be accused of stealing. What do you think the girl did? That's right. She cut the other ponytail off too.

So it was no surprise to Jonetta that her unemployed, uneducated daughter just gave birth to baby number four with her poor excuse for a husband, Owen, and now he was gone. Jonetta tried to warn her about having all these babies, but she just didn't listen.

"Well, I suggest that you definitely have a talk with them once they come home from school today. You can only keep up the charade for so long. Luckily they are young and resilient. Cornell will probably take it the hardest since he's the oldest. But they will be fine and so will you. Owen did your whole family a favor. You should see this as a blessing," Jonetta advised.

"Well, I don't," Colette sniffed. "I see it as being abandoned. I didn't sign up for this..."

"Oh, yes you did!" Jonetta interrupted. "Shall I remind you that you signed up for this life as soon as you decided to go against my will and move in with him? You were only eighteen-years-old, Colette. You were determined to be with this man, and now you have his children. You're bound to him for life. You signed up for it, alright. You marched yourself right into this situation. Nobody twisted your arm! But now you see that all that glitters ain't gold."

"Mama, I don't need this right now," Colette whined.

"What do you need, Colette?" Jonetta demanded and mashed her cigarette into a saucer. She smoked for enjoyment and was not about to waste another puff during this conversation.

Colette continued to sniff and sob. "I'm not sure. A gun, maybe? I want to blow his brains out! And that whore, Shante! I could kill them both!" Colette raged.

"Careful what you wish for," Jonetta admonished. She knew all about wishing someone dead.

"I'll call you tomorrow, mama," Colette replied.

"Don't do anything that you will regret! Just let the chips fall where they may. It's for the best. You'll see. Chin up," Jonetta tried her best to encourage her daughter. But she knew that she was failing miserably.

"Bye, mama."

Jonetta slapped her hand on her forehead and let out a long sigh. Colette's life was exhausting at times, and although she tried to talk sense into her, it seemed to escape her. There was nothing she could possibly do for her at this point, except help her with a few bills. Owen had been the worst decision of her young life and now with four children by him there was no escaping. Jonetta knew that Owen would be back sooner or later, as always. This was their merry-go-round soap opera, but Jonetta hoped Owen would be gone for good this time around.

Just as she rose from the table her phone rang again. This time it was her favorite daughter calling. She flashed a smile and answered happily, "Hello, baby! How are you?"

"Hey mama! I'm doing really good out here. I've got some really good news too!"

"What's that?"

"I'm coming home for Thanksgiving!" Dawn exclaimed.

"I can't wait, baby," Jonetta beamed. "We'll all be so happy to see you." She had not seen Dawn since last spring. Even then, it was a short visit because she was in Chicago on a photo shoot. "Will you be bringing Vine too?"

"Of course, he's coming home as well. Vine hasn't seen his family in two years. We're both really excited! Just when I was about to surprise him with plane tickets home for the holidays, he came home with some really surprising news for me," Dawn explained.

"Oh, really? Let me guess, he's going to be a leading man in a new movie," Jonetta teased. She really believed in her daughter's capabilities, but didn't know Vine well enough to entertain his dreams of becoming an actor.

"Actually, Vine was chosen to be on the TV series, 'The Haves and the Have Nots'," Dawn replied. "Mama, have you ever heard of it?"

"No, I haven't. What channel does it come on? You know I don't watch much television these days. I've been so busy back and forth..." Jonetta stopped herself from telling Dawn about Fred being in the hospital and her new living arrangements. She didn't want to spoil the moment because she could tell that Dawn was really excited.

"It comes on cable television. It's Tyler Perry's show," Dawn explained. "You do know who that is, don't you, mama?"

"Yes, of course, but I don't have cable. Anyway, I'm glad he landed a role on television. That stage play stuff will only take you so far."

"I agree, but that's his first love. Anyway, taping begins right after Thanksgiving, so we'll be flying in on Tuesday and leaving out on Saturday. I hope that's enough time to spend with you, mama," Dawn said. "Last time it was only a few hours so I really wanted to spend some days with you. I want to talk to you about things, so I hope to get you to myself at least for a little while."

"I'll make sure of that, don't worry. Anything for my baby," Jonetta reassured her. "But you'll be staying at Aunt Georgia's house when you come to town. I'll text the address and you can get a cab or Uber from the airport."

"Why am I staying with Aunt Georgia? I want to stay with you," Dawn whined.

"I'm staying here too," Jonetta sighed. Against her better judgment she brought Dawn up to speed on the circumstances as of late with Georgia and Fred.

"Wow! Poor Fred. I know aunt Georgia is just out of her mind right now. They have true love," Dawn sighed. "They have been together for decades. Those are definitely my relationship goals."

Jonetta rolled her eyes and sighed. She never really cared for her sister's interracial relationship. Not because she didn't like white people, because they were all in her family. And it certainly was not because Fred was an awful person, quite the contrary. Fred was a good man to Georgia. He was compassionate, generous and never made an issue about race. Jonetta was simply jealous that her efforts of dating white men never paid off.

"So how is everyone else?" Dawn inquired.

Jonetta sighed, "That's a loaded question. Where should I start?"

"I'll take the condensed, edited version at this point," Dawn laughed.

"Well, Owen has left Colette again, and I hope for good. Phyllis and Damien are moving again. But all of my grandchildren, remarkably, are doing just fine in all this chaos. Imagine that."

"Good grief! I'm sending positive energy to everyone right now. I'll have to give them a call and do some face time."

"Dawn, when you do, please don't let on that you know anything. You know how sensitive they are about somebody telling their business!"

Dawn laughed, "We're a family! What's with all the secrets?"

"Dawn, please," Jonetta admonished. "I don't want to any raucous around the holidays with everybody being emotional. You know how it is when a bunch of women come together. So, with that said, I welcome any male presence in this family to balance things out."

"Okay, mama. No worries. I'll play dumb," Dawn laughed. "Vine and I will see you in a few weeks. I love you."

"I love you too baby," Jonetta beamed. "I'll see you soon."

Jonetta put her phone on silent mode. She did not want anyone disturbing her peace for the remainder of the day. If at all possible.

7

Phyllis

As if things were not already stressful enough these past few weeks, Serena was sick and home from school. It was only a matter of days that Sabrina would get sick too. That's how it was with twins, if one got sick, the other would as well as if on cue. Damien took a few vacation days to finish packing, cleaning and finally moving into their new home this coming weekend, but he was spending most of his time taking care of Serena. Even though they had ample time before their lease was up Phyllis wanted to move as soon as possible since the holidays were approaching. She wanted her new house to be all set up with everything in place so when it was time to cook for Thanksgiving her house would be in order. Everything was going according to her plan until Serena came down with a chest cold. Serena was a daddy's girl and Damien soaked it up by pampering and cuddling her as if she were a new born baby. He was a good father so Phyllis tried not to complain, but she was tired of stacking boxes alone.

"Babe, do we have anymore soup?" Damien asked rummaging through the kitchen boxes.

"There should be some cans in the cabinet. Don't open those boxes!" she warned.

"Serena is hungry again. Where are the crackers?" He ignored Phyllis and began to open a box.

"Don't open the boxes, Damien, I swear!" Phyllis rushed to reseal the box. "If she's hungry that means she's getting better. Stop babying her all the time."

"What is your problem? Our daughter is sick and she's hungry. Now fix her some soup with crackers," Damien demanded and left the kitchen.

"Excuse me?" Phyllis quipped indignant with her hand on her hip.

Damien came back to the kitchen and glared at his wife. "You heard me. I'm sick of your attitude lately. You're pissed off because we have to move? So what! Get over it. That's not going to change the situation. It is what it is."

"It's your fault we have to move!" Phyllis lashed out.

"That fact doesn't change it either. So are you finished?" Damien blinked his eyes repeatedly and waited for an answer.

Phyllis didn't have a comeback. He was right. No matter how angry she was it did not change the fact that they still have to move. She reached for a can of chicken noodle soup and a pot that she left out to use until moving day. She felt him walk up behind her. He wrapped his hand around her waist.

"I'm sorry," Damien whispered in her ear. He swept her hair to the side and kissed her neck. "I'll make this up to you, I promise. It won't happen again. Next time we move it will be because we're buying our own home."

Phyllis nodded her head. One thing she knew for sure, this would not happen again. As soon as they got situated in their new house she was going to begin keeping up with all the bills whether Damien liked it or not. She had already found software online to install on her iPad to assist with monthly budgeting. Surely that would clear things up about how their money was being spent. That meant that Damien would need to give her access to all of his bank accounts and that would be a conversation to be had when had some liquor in him.

The pot of soup was boiling hot so Phyllis added a cup of water to it to cool it down. She reached in the box labeled Dry Foods to open a pack of Ritz Crackers. She opened the bottom cabinet where she hid a bottle of vodka way in the back. As soon as she was about to reach for it her smartphone rang. She glanced at it on the counter and saw her mother's picture on the screen. Her mother was the last person she wanted to hear from, she sighed and called for Damien to get the soup to Serena.

Phyllis handed him a plastic spoon and napkin, then held her phone up so he could see that her mother was on the phone and waved her hand at him to leave the kitchen. She answered dryly on the third ring, "Hello."

"Well, hello to you too! What bug is up your skirt?" Jonetta had the gift of picking up on moods from other people and especially her children. They could never fake it with her even when they wanted to pretend like everything was just fine.

"Mama, I'm just tired from packing and now Serena sick so you know that means Sabrina will be next. She'll be home from school soon worrying my nerves half to death too."

"I'm sorry Serena is sick, but that doesn't mean Sabrina has to get sick too. Just wipe everything down, keep them both medicated and make some soup. And once and for all quit complaining about the twins driving you crazy. You wanted children sooooo badly, remember?"

"I just gave Serena some chicken noodle soup..."

"From a can, I'm sure. That stuff is full of sodium. You should know better," Jonetta chided.

Phyllis took offense, "I do know better, thank you very much! I hardly have time to wipe my ass in privacy, let alone stand on my feet for four hours making homemade chicken soup."

"Hey! Watch your mouth, Phyllis," Jonetta chided.

Phyllis sighed and changed her tone, "Like I said we're in the middle of packing. Well, I'm in the middle of packing while Damien is busy being Mr. Mom pampering Serena when he actually could be lifting a damn box around here!"

"Well, I see that I've caught you at a bad time," Jonetta sound like her feelings were hurt. "I was just calling to see if you've heard from Colette lately."

Phyllis sucked her teeth.

"Yep, I heard from that heifer, and she was getting on my last nerves with all of her complaining."

"Well, go easy on her. You know she's having a tough time since Owen left her... again."

"Say what? She didn't tell me that!"

"Oh, dear, I shouldn't have said anything. I thought you knew."

"No, I didn't know. But now I do," Phyllis said, grinning. "Serves her ass right!"

"You and Colette really should just fight and get it over with! You've been at each other's throats since you were born," Phyllis remarked. "But it really isn't a surprise that he left again, after baby number four. Colette is just hard-headed. Well, I also wanted to let you know that Dawn will be home for the holidays."

Phyllis perked up just a little. She always enjoyed her baby sister when she came into town. They always found a way to go for mimosas at breakfast, happy hour or dancing at a night club when she was in town. Phyllis welcomed her company because it came with a change of pace and scenery outside of her boring routine.

"That's great news! I can't wait to see Dawn," Phyllis replied. "She's been blowing up on Instagram lately."

"On what?"

Phyllis heard Serena moaning from upstairs. "Never mind mama, I've gotta go now. It sounds like Serena needs me."

"Okay, kiss her for me, bye."

"Will do. Bye, mama," Phyllis ended the call and headed upstairs. This would be the last time for sickness in this house with her family. In a sense, she was grateful they were getting a fresh start, but the process was frustrating. Every time she put too much thought into it she grew angry so she wanted to focus on the new beginnings ahead. She grabbed the bottle of vodka, held it closely to her chest and began to unscrew the top. The fumes permeated through her nostrils and she smiled. As her lips touched the rim of the bottle she felt that familiar sting and quickly took a swig. She exhaled loudly with her head tilted backward.

"Babe!" Damien shouted.

"I'm right here!" She shouted back as she landed on the top step.

"She's got a fever and she just threw up all the soup," Damien reported frantically and pointed at the floor and his pants.

"Aww, my poor baby. Okay, let me get some towels," Phyllis headed to the linen closet in the hallway. She quickly separated the fancy towels from the inexpensive ones and something fell onto her foot. She looked down and saw that it was a Horseshoe Casino card. When she bent over to pick it up Damien entered the hallway demanding to know what was taking so long.

Phyllis spun around with the towel in one hand and the casino card in the other. Her chest heaved and the alcohol began escaping through her pores. Sweat began forming underneath her wire bra just like when she was in Zumba class. Now she regretted taking that swig of vodka. She needed her bearings about her now that she discovered Damien was wasting all of their money at a casino. It all made sense, all the money unaccounted for, the excuses then the lack of excuses, and all the time spent with his friends every pay day. Damien was a compulsive gambler.

She cocked her head to the side and shouted, "Really?!" Phyllis threw the towel at him. "Here! Go clean yourself up and I'll see to Serena." She grabbed a paper towel roll from the top shelf and few more towels and pushed past him in the hallway.

"Baby, let me explain," he pleaded.

"We'll talk about this later," Phyllis replied holding up the casino card in his face. She slid it in her back pocket for safekeeping. Upon entering the room her anger subsided when she saw how pitiful her daughter looked laying in the bed. Phyllis felt her forehead and it was hot. She kissed her forehead and said, "That's from grandma." Then she kissed her cheek and said, "That's from me. Mommy is going to get you well."

Phyllis began wiping up the chicken noodle soup that looked exactly as it did when it came out of the can. Serena had barely chewed at all. She had been scarfing down food like that since she was a toddler. Sabrina on the other hand always took her slow time eating. They were total opposites, but it suited them. Whenever Serena was upset, Sabrina would calm her. Whenever Sabrina would act too shy Serena would urge her to be more social. Damien would tease them calling them his Ying Yang Twins. But everyone affectionately called them Beena and Reena. Names they came up with as toddlers because they couldn't pronounce each other's names yet.

Serena coughed painfully, then asked, "Where's Beena?"

Phyllis looked at her watch and shouted to Damien, "The bus will be pulling up any minute! Can you go out to the curb and meet Sabrina?"

"I'm on it! Just changing my pants," he shouted back from their bedroom.

Phyllis rolled her eyes, but flashed a smile to Serena. "Let's get you cleaned up, baby."

"Mommy, are you and daddy..." she coughed again. "Fighting? Are you mad at me?"

Phyllis rushed to her side, "Oh, no baby! We're not mad at you. We're not fighting. We love you very much and we're going to make you feel better." Phyllis smoothed Serena's hair and caressed her face. "You're burning up. Let me get your medicine."

She caught a glimpse of Damien rushing down the stairs. She wanted to give him a swift kick just to help him hurry along. Phyllis shook her head as she walked to the main bathroom and reached in the medicine cabinet to grab the Children's Motrin. She closed the cabinet door and looked at herself in the mirror. For a moment she was ready to beat herself up for being so stupid for not noticing Damien's gambling habits before, but decided against it. As far as she was concerned, this was his fault. All his doing and he was going to fix it and fast.

Once Serena was settled and Sabrina was done with homework and fed, Phyllis decided to confront Damien. She had knots in her stomach at the thought of how long he was addicted to gambling. As she approached their bedroom Damien looked up from where he was standing in front of the mirror and they locked eyes. Phyllis wanted to shave his beautiful locs right from his head as a punishment, but his eyes were pleading for her forgiveness.

Damien turned towards her and rested on the edge of the dresser as if bracing for the verbal storm that was about to thrash him.

"So, Mr. Damien, Casino King," Phyllis snarled as she entered their bedroom lightly closing the door behind her. "I guess you should begin with the telling me the truth, finally."

"Babe," he sighed.

Phyllis held up her hand, "No, don't call me babe! Not tonight." She placed her hands on her hips and waited for him to proceed. There was a long pause. Phyllis raised her eyebrows in anticipation for her husband to say something, anything.

"I'm going to make it right, I promise," Damien said. He stood up straight and began to walk towards Phyllis. It was typical of him to try to touch her when he was in hot water. Sometimes it worked, but Phyllis wasn't falling for it this time. She retreated and sat on the edge of their king size bed.

"Okay, since you're not going to offer up the truth I guess I have to ask one hundred questions. So let's begin with what I discovered today. Why was that casino card stuffed between the towels in my linen closet?"

"Remember that day you were rushing me to take the clothes to the cleaners? I checked the pockets of my pants and found it. I just put it in the nearest place I could think of because you were coming up the steps." Damien shrugged. "I totally forgot I put it there."

"How long have you been an addict?"

"An addict? I'm not an addict, Phyllis!" Damien refuted. "Don't go dramatizing this into some Lifetime movie, alright?"

"Damien, the way I see how our finances have dwindled, how you can't maintain paying bills on time and now we have to move. I'd say you're pretty much a compulsive gambler! In other words, an addict!" Phyllis stood her ground. "So I'm going to ask you again, how long have you been addicted to gambling?"

Damien exhaled and replied, "I've been gambling since I was a teenager, Phyllis. It started out with shooting dice, you know, nothing serious. Then in my twenties I began going to Indiana to play at the casino, just the slots, and roulette. Then I learned how to play poker with the fellas, and I was good. Then that progressed into playing the tables at the casino. I had my good days and my bad days. But I have it under control, babe."

Phyllis shot him a look of disapproval. "You are delusional if you think that you have your gambling under control. Not only are you throwing away our money, you're also burning gas money driving back and forth to Indiana! Look at the constant financial uncertainty and strain we're in all the time! I've had to ask my mother for money for us, do you know how humiliating that is? I've even come close to asking my father for money a time or two, but I knew that would crush your foolish pride if I took that route. I've been out here begging family just so we can stay afloat and all along you've been throwing it to the wind like you're some kind of big shot! You drive a damn UPS truck for crying out loud! How could you be so selfish and stupid? So how much money have you lost since we've been together?"

"I don't know!" Damien exclaimed and began walking back and forth. He looked as if he was trying to calculate it all in his head.

"Take a damn guess then!" Phyllis insisted. "And you're in no position to shout at me!"

Damien sighed, "Phyllis, honestly..."

"Damien Xavier Washington, I swear if you don't give me a damn dollar figure..."

"What difference does it make, huh?" Damien demanded. "Is the dollar amount going to determine if you are going to leave me or something?"

"Maybe," Phyllis replied and pursed her lips. "Just tell me!"

"Since we've met?" Damien stalled. He stuffed his hands in his pockets and shrugged.

"Yes, that's what I asked," Phyllis tried to remain calm. Her lips tightened and her chest heaved as she sat almost frozen on their bed.

"Since we've met I've *gained* and lost. How do you think I paid for our vacations? Certainly not from tips or bonus money on the job. I don't recall you complaining when we're having fun, shopping, or splurging at Christmas and for all of our birthdays," Damien countered.

"I asked about losses."

"Well, um, if I had to guess, I'd say roughly, about ten or fifteen," Damien rubbed his beard. He stared at his wife waiting for her reaction.

Phyllis sat in silence. Her eyes darted back and forth. She was trying to do the calculations in her head with that dollar figure. It still didn't add up to her.

"Seems like it would be more than that over the years," Phyllis said out loud more to herself than Damien. "How long have we been together Damien?"

"Eleven years."

"I don't remember having money troubles before the twins were born, do you?"

"No, not really. But then again, you were working then."

"I quit my job so we could *save* money on daycare expenses," Phyllis reminded him. "All this time I thought the twins' expenses were killing our pockets, and that maybe I should go back to work. But it's been you just tossing your hard earned money to the casino without a care in the world."

"You make it seem like I was just digging in my pockets every chance I got and rushing to gamble. If you haven't noticed, I'm actually home more lately. I knew my gambling was becoming a problem. I'm sorry for hiding it all these years. But I was trying to fix it. I still am trying to fix it!"

"Do you owe anybody any money? Are we in trouble? And don't lie to me, Damien!"

"No, I'm not in any debt to anybody, thankfully."

"I would hope you'd let me know if our lives were in danger," Phyllis retorted and rolled her eyes. She sighed and stretched out on the bed. "I have a headache now."

"I'll get you some Tylenol," Damien offered.

"That's not what I need," Phyllis shot back.

"Well, what do you need?"

"A new life."

8

Dawn

As the weeks rolled by, Dawn prepared for her trip back home to Chicago. Although the weather had been mild for October in New York, she convinced herself that she needed to go shopping for fall clothing, jackets and boots for the weather in Chicago. Not that she needed any new clothes because there were plenty in her closet with the price tags still dangling from them. But really she was using retail therapy as a way to lick her fresh wounds that were complimentary from Vine. She had finally told him about the plane tickets to Chicago and although he had to adjust his schedule at the café, he was still excited to go back home to see his family for the holidays. But the days conflicted with filming in Atlanta so he would only be able to visit for one day, Thanksgiving Day.

Dawn did not complain about the scheduling conflict, but secretly she wished they would cancel or reschedule so he could be with her for the holidays. Since nobody ever believed that their relationship would last more than a few months, she wanted to gloat and show off a bit in front of everyone. Not to mention brag on her man's opportunity of a lifetime filming for Tyler Perry. They have been together for three years going strong and that was something for Dawn to be proud of too. The family could always count on Dawn bringing a different guy around for almost every holiday function. She would get what she needed from each relationship and keep it moving until the next one came along. But not this time. She was in love.

Her smartphone alerted that she had a new message from Facebook. She finished folding a sweater then reached for it on the night stand next to their bed. A smile grew across her face as she read the message from her sister Colette. Finally, she created a page somewhere on social media. Dawn responded aloud as she typed on her smartphone, "It's about time girl! Welcome to the twenty first century!"

Vine poked his head in the room and asked, "Who's that you're talking to? And are you going somewhere?" Vine looked confused about the suitcase being wide open on their bed.

"Yes, to Chicago, remember? I'm just trying to decide what to take with me, that's all. My sister, Colette, finally got on Facebook," she replied grinning. "I'll have to send her some pics of herself because this profile picture is not doing her any justice."

"Well, at least you get to see recent pics of your nieces and nephew now," Vine said.

"I sure can," Dawn agreed. "I just hope she doesn't use this as a sounding board to tell all of her business. You know that she always has some type of drama going on with that man of hers."

Vine chuckled and coughed.

"It's not that funny," Dawn said and frowned at him.

"No, no, my throat is a little sore that's all. I may need some medicine to soothe it before it gets any worse," he explained. "You've been sleeping with that fan and the temperature is dropping so it's been a little chilly in here at night."

"Well, why didn't you say something?"

Vine shot her a look of disbelief. "Really, babe?"

Dawn sat wide eyed but conceded quickly, "Alright, alright, I won't use it unless it's necessary."

"Have you had any nightmares lately?" Vine asked genuinely concerned.

"Not in the past few weeks, but now since you've brought it up, I'm sure that I'll have one tonight," Dawn said flippantly.

"I still think you should see somebody about that. Maybe even a session of hypnosis will help to get to the bottom of the wicked old lady."

"Poke fun all you want, but I'll pass on that," Dawn sneered at him. "And for your information, it's not a wicked old lady in my nightmares. She's just an old white lady struggling to get a pillow off of her face. The person smothering her is just a dark figure and I'm just standing there witnessing this in horror. Anyway, I plan on asking my mom when I get back home if there's any significance to it."

Vine leaned down to kiss her forehead, "Good idea. In the meantime, you need to get in that kitchen and make your man some hot, homemade chicken soup to heal his body."

"Oh yeah?" Dawn pulled his face towards hers. "I got something else that's nice and hot that will heal your body." She kissed his lips, but he pulled away holding her hands.

"Babe, I don't want to pass my germs to you," Vine kissed her hands. "Besides, I've got to get to work."

"It's only a quarter past five! You've got some time," Dawn whined. "And you can afford to be late unless you're trying to earn Employee of the Month at the café?" She teased.

On that note Vine told her that he would see her later, left the bedroom and closed the door behind him. Dawn sat baffled but decided to text him to get to the bottom of his emotions regarding that café.

> Dawn: *Why did you leave like that?*
> Vine: *You just don't get it.*
> Dawn: *Get What???*

Dawn waited patiently for his response, but didn't receive one. Completely disgusted, she tossed the phone on the bed.

She opened the nightstand drawer looking for her joint, but didn't find one and slammed the drawer closed. The next best thing would be a shot of tequila, but she knew they didn't keep any in the house. Dawn marched to the kitchen, yanked open the refrigerator hoping to at least find a bottle of wine. No luck. But what she did notice was their refrigerator was stocked with different bags of fresh ground coffee. French roast, Vanilla, Chai, Columbian, and one from Spain. She slammed the door closed and scanned the kitchen counter for a bottle of vodka at least. Nothing.

Their counter was cluttered with utensils, knives, spices, and two different coffee makers. One traditional pot, the kind her mother had, and one state-of-the-art automatic maker that also made tea. Dawn scoffed, and shook her head. She didn't want any of that. Until now, she had never realized just how much Vine loved coffee. Why is their apartment full of things that he likes to drink? Where were her favorite drinks? She had a mind to toss all the ground coffee in the garbage to teach him a lesson, but thought better of it. That would certainly start a war and she wanted to be at peace with him especially around the holidays.

Vine had his nerve being in his feelings about her comment, it's not like he's trying to make a career out of being a barista. He's a rising star with acting opportunities knocking at his door. Dawn had to come up with a way for him to see that his true passion was acting and that his sensitivity about the café was simply unnecessary.

Her smartphone made a noise and she went dashing back into the bedroom for it.

"He better had," she said aloud grinning. She let out a deep sigh. It was not a message from Vine, but rather her friend, Kara, asking to meet for drinks in SoHo. Dawn wasn't on shift at the bar tonight, so why not? That's exactly what she needed.

As she sifted through her clothes that were cramped in the small closet she thought of donating the clothes to a women's shelter, but quickly thought better of it. What would they know about properly caring for quality clothes? If her sisters were a smaller size Dawn would definitely pass the clothes to them, but Colette has been out of shape since her second child. Phyllis is petite, but curvy. Maybe she would pack some clothes for her sister to get tailored. Maybe.

Dawn reached for an emerald green cashmere V-neck sweater that revealed cleavage. The skinny jeans she had on cupped her butt just right so she decided to wear them. She slipped on her UGG boots, grabbed her burnt orange cloak, and threw on her Louis Vuitton Sunglasses. As usual she did a mirror check, snapped a selfie for Instagram, posted it and headed out the door.

The sunlight greeted her the moment she had stepped outside and seemed to follow her until she went underground to catch the subway. Her mood was always lifted whenever the sun decided to show its face and this was the last little bit of it for the day. She stood on the crowded train all the way to her final stop. It was something she adapted to, even while wearing heels, thanks to one incident when chewing gum that was stuck on the side of her seat somehow latched onto her Valentino slacks. Since then Dawn only rode the subway standing regardless of empty seats available. She reached into her pants pocket for her iPhone 6S and was bummed that Vine had not responded yet.

The computerized voice came across the train car announcing her stop in SoHo was next and she smiled to herself. Between Midtown, Greenwich Village, and SoHo she passed up well over 100 bars, but she didn't feel like dressing up. At this particular bar, The Lazy Point, she knew a Whiskey Sour was awaiting her and she couldn't wait to order it, drink it and be in a better mood.

Vine had seemed unhappy with her lately and she needed a way to fix it. As she walked briskly a few blocks to the bar, her mind wandered back and forth between her and Vine. Maybe she talked too much. Maybe she should not always speak her mind. But then again, Dawn was not the one to walk around on eggshells for anyone. She always said exactly how she felt to a fault. It struck a nerve with her that Vine refused to communicate exactly what bothered him. She hated it when he behaved like a childish little girl. He couldn't help it, she supposed, being raised by women will do that to a man. God forbid if she ever brought that up, he would catch an attitude and be in his feelings. The uncertainty of their relationship had always caused Dawn to retract and become withdrawn. She hated feeling like a fool. That's exactly how she felt now since Vine still had not returned her text.

Once she got off the train and walked up to the street level the sun had bid its farewell and gave way to the moon. Dawn checked her smartphone one more time before entering the bar. There still wasn't a text from Vine. Dawn mashed her lips together and exhaled. Not a sigh of defeat, but rather that one of accepting a challenge. Nobody could play the ignore game better than Dawn. If that's how Vine wanted it, she was game.

After round three of drinks and one round of complimentary shots from a group of unknown men, Dawn and Kara decided to order Fingerling Potato Tempura to soak up some of the alcohol. Dawn felt her feet floating and knew it would only be a matter of time before she was dancing on top of a bar.

"It's so good catching up with you, Dawn," Kara slurred. "I've missed you!" She slung her long thin arm around her shoulder and nuzzled her head against Dawn's. Kara was also a happy transplant from Philadelphia. The two had met at fashion show where they literally bumped heads while undressing backstage. Dawn was perturbed by it, but Kara made light of it and they've been close ever since. Kara was the same height but pale in complexion with long wavy light brown hair. She could almost pass for white, but she was biracial.

Once she began talking it was evident that she was raised with an ethnic background. Initially Dawn was cautious of Kara simply because it was New York. The city was full of grimy people who only looked out for themselves. But once she learned that Kara was from Philadelphia, the city of Brotherly Love, she was more open to getting to know her. Besides New York was a lonely place without friends and family. Since Dawn was not into smothering her man, she would often explore New York City alone.

"All you have to do is call," Dawn patted her cheek and released her hold. The last thing she wanted was puke all over her sweater. Kara was cute and all, but if she lost her cookies all over Dawn it was not going to be a good look for either of them.

"Well, you've been so wrapped up in your boo..."

"Don't even try it," Dawn interrupted her. One thing was certain Dawn was not that type to forsake her friends for a man. Men always came and went, but she valued friendships.

The waitress placed the tempura potatoes on the table and they dove in before she could place the utensils and plates down. Dawn had not indulged in fried foods for so long she had forgotten how delicious it tasted.

"You sent a text. I came to hang out. That's all it takes," Dawn said and licked her fingers.

"I hear you girl," Kara grinned and stuffed two potatoes into her mouth. She reached for a glass of water and chugged it down. "I needed that!"

Dawn suggested that they head home while they still had their bearings about them and before the men gained too much confidence. They paid their tab, locked arms and walked as briskly as they could to the subway. Dawn could hear her mother's words of wisdom: "Walk with purpose and nobody will mess with you." That was sound advice that she gave Dawn prior to her move to New York. It made sense and even now she moved as swiftly as she could although the alcohol was winning as it took over her limbs. Her feet felt like they were stuck in thick mud, but when she glanced down they were moving right along.

Kara giggled as they collided into each other. "We might as well be doing a three legged race!"

"I'm trying to hold onto you for your sake," Dawn laughed. "And mine."

"We suck big time! We're sloppy drunk." Kara giggled. "I'm going to take the train to your house and catch a cab back to my place."

"That makes no sense," Dawn said, stopping in her tracks and waving Kara off. "You're going to pass up your place..."

"We are each other's keeper," Kara slurred her words. "Now, shh-hh...and follow me."

Dawn shrugged. She was in no mood to argue. But she did feel comforted by having Kara accompany her on the train ride home. Two drunk chicks were safer than one riding public transportation alone, Dawn figured.

On the train Dawn rested her head on Kara's shoulder. "I'm so mad at Vine," she confessed.

"Why?" Kara inquired. She could only manage that one word with her eyes closed.

Dawn exhaled. "I don't know. Seems like we're drifting apart and I don't know how to draw us back in," she replied and shut her eyes tight. "He didn't return my text message at all. It's been hours. That's so unlike him." Dawn absolutely hated admitting defeat in any situation, but especially when it came to her relationships with men.

Kara didn't have a response and Dawn wondered if it was because she was drunk or if she didn't think it was worth talking about. Ever since they met she had not known Kara to have one serious relationship. Whenever Dawn would mention any man, Kara would change the subject or get quiet. She was gorgeous, any man would love to have her, but Kara was aloof when it came to committing to a relationship.

The computerized voice announced over the intercom their stop would be next.

"C'mon," Kara said and shrugged her shoulder to get Dawn moving. "This is your stop, sweetie. Let's walk and talk."

Dawn slowly rose to her feet, thankful that she wore her boots instead of heels. The train jerked and Dawn stumbled into another passenger. "Oh, excuse me," she said and giggled.

"I gotcha," Kara said and grabbed her elbow. She led them off the train and to Dawn's apartment.

Dawn headed straight to her bedroom and threw herself across the bed face down. She heard water running in the kitchen and glasses clinking.

"Here's some water for both of us," Kara said and handed a glass of water to Dawn. They both needed it from all the shots that they were throwing back. Dawn obliged, sat up long enough to take a gulp.

Immediately she lied back down and instructed Kara to turn off the lights.

Kara removed the suitcase from the bed where Dawn had left it earlier. She flipped the switch on the wall and found her way to the bed.

"Going somewhere?" Kara inquired.

Dawn moaned and replied, "Home."

Kara plopped on the bed and stretched out next to Dawn. They both moaned. Dawn moaned from feeling nauseous more than she usually would. She threw her hand over her eyes.

"Oh, right. You're going home to Chicago for Thanksgiving," Kara sighed. "That must be nice. I wish that I could go home, well, at least to a happy home for the holidays."

"Kara," Dawn muttered. "Shhhhh... please. My head is spinning. Aren't you wasted?"

"I'm a little tipsy," she giggled. "But then again, I can drink most men under the table." Kara rolled onto her side and now she was facing Dawn. She smoothed back her fluffy, curly hair so that she could see her face. "I'm going to call Uber in a minute."

"Mmmkay," Dawn managed a reply.

"But about Vine," Kara spoke at a whisper. "I don't think he's manly enough for you, hunny bun. He seems passive and emotional. You need someone who will be assertive and aggressive with you. I know that shit turns you on."

Dawn sighed, "So you're not gonna shut up?"

Kara laughed, "I just wanted to say that before I forgot. It's no telling when I'm gonna see you again, missy."

Dawn turned over on her back and raised her eyebrows with her eyes still closed. "I love him, Kara."

"But does he love you? I mean, the *real* you. The side of you that you allow me to see, the side that you hide from him."

"He doesn't need to know everything, Kara," Dawn replied and placed her hand on her forehead.

Kara rose up on her elbows and stared at Dawn for a minute. She leaned down and placed her lips on top of Dawn's.

Dawn's eyes flew open. Still too disoriented to react quickly she could only manage a gasp. "What are you doing?" Dawn demanded and jerked her head away.

"What I've wanted to do since the day I met you, Dawn."

"Kara..." Dawn said and shook her head. She was about to sit up, but Kara pushed her shoulders back down.

"Just relax," Kara instructed. "I slipped you a little something to help ease and relax you so you can enjoy what I'm about to do to your sexy ass." She quickly climbed on top of Dawn, pulled her sweater up and unclasped her bra in the front in one quick motion. The next thing Dawn knew her breasts were in the mouth of a woman. Kara put all of her weight on top of Dawn that she was pinned down and too drunk and apparently drugged to fight her off.

"No! Stop it, Kara!" Dawn exclaimed. She took the palm of her hand and pushed Kara's face as hard as she could away from her. But her mouth was locked on her nipple and she had a strong pull on it.

Kara grabbed Dawn's hands, held them above her head by the wrists and smiled, "Putting up a fight only turns me on, Dawn."

"Bitch! Get off of me!"

Kara ignored her and began to unzip her skinny jeans. "You looked so damn good when you walked into the bar tonight. I wanted to taste you right then and there," Kara confessed. "All those men just chomping at the bit to get near you, but I knew you were gonna be mine tonight."

She released Dawn's hands to yank her pants down to her hips. Dawn struggled with one hand to keep her pants up while she grabbed a clump of Kara's hair just as she was about to put her face between her legs.

The bedroom light came on suddenly.

"What the hell is going on in here?!" Vine shouted.

9

Colette

Colette struggled to catch her breath. She gasped for air, but there was none. At first she thought it was just a nightmare, but her incessant coughing woke her up. She kept coughing. Finally, she took a deep breath, tasting the bitterness in the air. Her eyes flew open to witness smoke filtering into her bedroom. As if on cue she heard sirens blaring and getting closer. She wasn't just dreaming about choking this was really happening. There was a fire somewhere.

Colette sprung from her bed and opened her door to witness flames coming from the kitchen. They were dancing on the ceiling, reaching towards the dining room where her baby slept. She ran towards Delilah's crib, bundled her up in a blanket and ran down the hall to her children's bedroom.

"Wake up!" Colette screamed. "Kids! Wake up!"

She snatched the blankets off the girls and shook Cornell as hard as she could. "Get up! It's a fire! Get up! Let's go now!"

She heard pounding at her front door. Someone was shouting but she couldn't make out what they were saying. Delilah began to cry in her arms. The smoke began to fill the hallway and filter into the kids' bedroom.

"Girls, please get up!" Colette said between coughs. Her eyes burned and began to well up. She coughed and peeled back the baby blanket to check on Delilah. The baby was fine just probably scared and confused like the rest of them.

Ruthie began to cry when she saw the smoke. Lydia sat frozen in the corner of the bed. They all were coughing now as the smoke began to fill the small apartment. The more that they heard pounding on the door and more shouting from the hallway, the more they became stricken with fear. Cornell covered his mouth and began looking for his shoes.

"Cornell, baby, go open the front door, and hurry!"

"But mama, I can't see, my eyes are burning," he whined.

"I need you to be a big boy!" Colette shouted at him. Her eyes were burning too. She could barely breathe. "Run! Go open the door, Cornell!" He ran past her coughing and covering his eyes with his hand.

"Lydia! Let's go, now!" Colette snatched her by her foot and dragged her out of the bed with her one free hand.

Ruthie was holding onto her leg crying. "Run Ruthie! Get out of here! Go outside now!" She cried in fear, but did as she was told and disappeared into the smoke.

Colette clutched Delilah closer to her chest as she struggled to get Lydia to her feet. This child was always so stubborn, but now was certainly not the time. It was a matter of life or death so even if Colette had to drag Lydia out of the burning apartment by her ponytail she was willing to do just that.

"Baby, we have to go now!" She kept trying to gasp for fresh air to breathe, but it was pointless because the smoke had dominated the whole apartment.

Just then she felt someone grab her shoulder and push her towards the front door.

"Get out of here, Colette! I'll get Lydia." It was her elderly neighbor, Mr. Green. "Nobody's dying tonight!"

Colette ran towards the front door as fast as she could. She held her breath and her baby who was screaming to the top of her tiny lungs with her eyes squinted. The smoke had become thick within a matter of minutes. She was so relieved that Mr. Green came to their rescue. He was always helping out anytime he could with her children. He even would make sure they walked to and from school safely when Owen was too drunk or when she was too exhausted from being pregnant. Now she trusted Mr. Green to get her baby out of that apartment safely. Tears ran down her face from fear and the singe of the smoke.

She bumped into firemen into the hallway. They ordered her down the stairs, but she wouldn't leave until she saw Mr. Green and Lydia come out of the apartment alive. As if they knew she wasn't going to comply with their orders another fire fighter took Delilah from her arms and escorted them down the stairs and outside.

"Cornell! Ruthie! Where are you?" She could barely feel her feet moving, but she knew they were because now she was outside amongst a crowd. Her heart raced as she scanned the crowd looking for her son and daughter. She called out their names again.

"Where are my children?" Colette screamed.

"They're over here, ma'am," the fire fighter said and walked her towards the ambulance.

Colette threw her arms around them both and fell to her knees sobbing. The paramedic had Delilah inside checking her for smoke inhalation. Another paramedic updated her on the status of all her children and they seemed to be fine, but she advised that they still go to the hospital for examinations. Colette's head was spinning, she sobbed and coughed. She could barely form a sentence to respond to the paramedic.

"We need to check you too, ma'am," the paramedic said and tried to help Colette to her feet.

Suddenly she heard applause and cheering from the crowd. "Everybody's out. All clear. Over." A fireman's voice reported over the walkie-talkie two-way.

She stood up to see Mr. Green, and a fire fighter carrying Lydia coming out of the building. Mr. Green was bent over covering his mouth with a handkerchief. The fire fighter was rushing Lydia to the adjacent ambulance. Her body was limp. Colette took off running.

"Ma'am, please allow us to do our job," a male paramedic said struggling to get Lydia, who needed immediate attention, inside the ambulance. "Ma'am, please!"

"My baby!" She screamed in horror.

10

Phyllis

Only three weeks in their new house and Phyllis was already complaining about how small it was, the lack of space, and how they need to buy their own home sooner than later. She hoped that Damien would get the hint, but he would never respond the way she had expected. Instead, he kept reminding her to just be thankful they could start somewhere fresh. But if it were not for his gambling addiction they would not have to start fresh somewhere else. It was a dead argument at this point. Phyllis bit her tongue on many occasions during the move, and she was proud of herself. Of course, taking swigs of vodka from a water bottle didn't hurt either.

It really annoyed Phyllis when she didn't have the time to decorate the house for Halloween, nor take the twins trick or treating. Unpacking and arranging their new house stole the joy right out of anything fun. Phyllis took great joy in choosing costumes, sprucing them up and putting make-up on the girls. All of the pictures she posted on social media got lots of views and comments on how cute her twins were and how creative she was with the costumes. It gave her a sense of pride and purpose. But not this year, and yes, that was Damien's fault too.

That wasn't a topic she was willing to discuss with him though. Phyllis knew that he would give a speech about how it's the devil's holiday anyway. About two years ago, Damien decided that he wasn't going to celebrate any pagan holidays. But yet, he was telling her what desserts he wanted for Thanksgiving. She didn't have the patience to go back and forth with him over his inconsistent beliefs. They had bigger fish to fry. Like how to repay her father for the money he loaned them for the move.

Phyllis had finally spoken to her father about their situation. Of course, as expected, he was not pleased. Being a man raised in the south he could not understand how Damien let it come to this.

"A man should take care of home first. Everything else is second," her father chided. "That's basic manhood shit! Who raised this clown?"

Phyllis knew that her father would go off, belittle her husband, and be downright insulting. All the reasons she dreaded ever calling him. Her father never had one kind word to say about Damien. According to her father, when they couldn't conceive, it was Damien's fault for smoking weed the majority of his life. When they needed help buying a new car, it was Damien's fault for not knowing how to fix the one they had. When he lost his job at the Ford Motor plant, it was his fault for not showing initiative that he could do more than work on an assembly line. The list went on and on, and although Phyllis hated to hear it, she had to swallow a gallon of pride this time to ask her father for money for moving expenses.

"Ain't this some shit?" Her father declared when Phyllis finally asked for his assistance. "Dammit! I hope y'all find a way to get out of this financial rut that you've been in for a decade now. Tell me something, and I mean tell it to me now, Phyllis Marie Miller Washington, are you all a bunch of crack heads in that house?"

"Dad, really?" Phyllis tried her best to remain respectful, but she was just about to lose her cool. She may over indulge on liquor every now and then, but one thing was for sure, she was never going to dabble into drugs, unlike other members in the family. Her father had just crossed the line and she wanted to tell him in a few choice words how much that just hurt. But she decided against it and remained respectful. "That's pretty insulting and farfetched, don't you think?"

"No, not really," he replied indignant. "Here's why, y'all are always moving, you can't keep a car or a roof over your head without a perfectly good explanation. And y'all are always begging for money just to make ends meet. Your mama told me she had to buy you groceries at one point just so your kids could have a home cooked meal for a change. But from what I hear, your ass don't ever cook anyway! Then I hear that you all go on vacations and have lavish birthday parties for the twins. All the money is being spent on something foolish. Y'all have a hole in your pocket soon as the money hits! It's crack-ish behavior. If it's not crack then it sounds like somebody has another bad habit that they can't AFFORD so it's time to let it loose! Because coming to me or your mama asking for money or food or whatever is not a good look for two grown ass people. Do I look like the National Bank of the Miller's to you? Dammit! I have a life too, ya know? All the money that I've dished out to y'all two irresponsible, grown ass, adults over the past few years could've bought me a damn villa in the Bahamas by now. Shit! I worked hard for my money all these years. I saved. I invested. I had a damn end goal in mind. What's your end goal? I kept the same damn job at the steel mill until they shut it down. I put in my time. I took care of my family. What's Damien's excuse?"

Phyllis remained quiet or so it seemed. She had actually hit the mute button while her father went on a tirade. A glass of vodka on the rocks with a splash of pineapple juice was in her hand. She rolled her eyes, took a sip and shook her head as he gave this speech. There was the bomb she was avoiding, but it had just dropped and exploded.

"Hello? I asked a god-damned question!" He shouted.

Phyllis hit the mute button again and replied, "I'm here, dad. I don't know what his excuse is, I really don't." She placed the glass down on the kitchen table so her father wouldn't hear the ice clinking as she walked back and forth. It seemed to help her stay focused.

"Well, that's another fault of yours as his wife! It's your job to track the money especially if you're not working. You're just living on the edge otherwise by allowing someone to control your life and future! You were raised better than this. You're smarter than this, Phyllis."

"You're right, dad," she conceded. "I already have a plan in motion to do better with our budget because it is humiliating asking my parents for help when I have a husband."

"Well, good. I'm glad to hear it. So when do you plan on taking your ass back to work? This isn't all on Damien. You have a responsibility as well to keep your family on their feet just as much as he does. This ain't the damn sixties, girl. Women work these days because the cost of living takes two capable working adults with a family to keep from falling off a financial cliff. I mean, too late for y'all ass, but you can always recover. That's gonna require some effort on your part too."

"You're right dad," Phyllis replied quickly. She picked up her glass again and took a sip. The idea of returning to work was never in her intentions. But she didn't want to engage in that battle of conversation with her father right now. She just needed him to agree to send the money so they could move.

"Don't be trying to shut me up by agreeing with me," her father chided. "You women got that down pat, dontcha? I ain't no god-damned fool, ya know?"

Phyllis chuckled, "Dad, I'm not trying to pacify you nor shut you up. I'm agreeing with you. I swear."

After he calmed down, they began talking about the twins and their schooling as of late. He always doted over his twin granddaughters, but they've only seen him three times since they were born. He admitted that as a grandfather that he needed to do better. Phyllis was happy to hear him acknowledge that he needed to be more present in all of their lives. By the time they ended their conversation, Phyllis was on her second glass of vodka.

Her father came through with the money the next day, but not without wanting to speak to Damien first. Phyllis asked what the conversation was about, but Damien was vague. She figured it may have hurt his pride, so she didn't press the issue. The only good thing was the twins were happy only because it was something new. They loved their new room, the backyard and their play room. Instead of having separate bedrooms Phyllis allowed the twins to share a bedroom and convert the spare room into a play room.

Damien seemed pleased with their new home, but Phyllis reminded him that this move was temporary. Although it was spacious enough for them, the house didn't have a basement. Phyllis needed a place to call her own, but couldn't find a spot in this house just yet. She needed to unwind with her favorite vodka in her favorite recliner. Right now it was in the living room, a community space, where she could easily be disturbed.

Phyllis stood in the living room and thought about how she could rearrange the furniture when she felt Damien wrap his arms around her waist. She exhaled. It had been weeks since she felt his warmth. They slept in the same bed but separate. His touch was only welcomed when and if she invited it. Lately, Damien knew that he was in the dog house so he didn't even try. But seeing her standing there in complete silence turned him on.

Damien couldn't help but wrap his arms around her. The tight yoga pants that accented her plump butt with an off the shoulder sweatshirt that exposed her bare right shoulder enticed him. He especially loved her sandy brown and blonde faux locs that hung past her shoulders. When Phyllis realized that they had extra money left she managed to squeeze in time to get her hair done just like Damien's. She had always admired how healthy and long his locs grew, but she wasn't brave enough to commit to the style.

He was thrilled when he saw the style on her. Damien said it favored Lisa Bonet's style, but Phyllis begged to differ. It turned him on even more and since then he's been trying to get at her. Damien slid his hands up and down her hips. Those hips that he loved to watch sway whenever she walked away.

Phyllis placed her hands on top of his and squeezed. Relieved by her acceptance, Damien leaned down, nuzzled his head in the curve of her neck and kissed it tenderly. Phyllis closed her eyes and moaned.

"I miss you," she admitted.

"We miss you too," Damien said and pressed his pelvis into her backside.

That turned her on completely. She turned to face him, lunged in to kiss him passionately and grabbed a handful of his locs. He welcomed her lips and pulled her faux locs. It was their thing. A signal to each other that sparks were about to fly. That passion was about to ensue and making love would be next.

"Ewww!" The twins simultaneously expressed their disgust. They were peeking around the corner.

Phyllis laughed, covered her mouth and whispered to Damien, "Fix yourself before you turn around." She patted his very erect manhood.

She chased them down the hall to distract them from seeing their father's manhood at full attention in his sweat pants. The girls squealed and ran into their room.

"What's so 'ewww' about mommy and daddy kissing, huh?"

Serena ran to Phyllis and hugged her. "Mommy, can you play dolls with us?"

"Yes! Say yes! Mommy, come on," Sabrina said and pulled Phyllis by the hand into their playroom. She couldn't deny their beaming faces and followed their lead. As they went from one room to the next she caught a glimpse of Damien standing in the hallway. He threw his hands in the air in disbelief. Phyllis shrugged and went happily in the room to play with her daughters.

"Okay...So I guess I'll just start dinner then!" Damien hollered.

"Sure, go ahead babe," Phyllis shouted back. If someone was going to be disappointed, it was not going to be her babies. As much as she prayed, cried and begged to become a mother, the twins got her full attention especially when they demanded it.

The girls strategically pulled dolls from their toy chest and immediately placed them in their doll house. Phyllis sat on the floor and helped them arrange the furniture in the doll house. Pots and pans were clanging in the kitchen because Damien was clearly upset that their special moment came to an abrupt halt. He could be a bigger baby than the twins when he wanted. Phyllis smirked to herself because she knew that once the twins were asleep he would only be more aggressive with her later on in the bedroom. It excited her when Damien fussed and became rough with her, so she allowed him to have a little temper tantrum now because it would pay off later.

Serena fussed at her sister for not keeping up with the dolls accessories. Phyllis tried to keep the peace, but Serena was very adamant. She was very organized for a five-year-old and liked getting her point across without interruption, much like Phyllis. Sabrina searched for the missing red shoe of one of the dolls in the toy chest.

"I don't know where it is, Reena!" Sabrina whined.

"That's why you should put it in the right place!" Serena exclaimed frustrated.

"Girls, please. Just choose another outfit and shoes for this doll," Phyllis's plea fell on deaf ears as the girls searched for the missing shoe.

Phyllis took a deep breath and the aromas of onions, garlic and bell peppers filled the air and teased her nose. She knew that Damien was about to make his famous lasagna that they loved so much. One of the ways Damien had won her over was by cooking for her on a regular basis. They began like any other couple, going out on dates to restaurants, but Damien was always bragging about how he could have made the food taste better. It wasn't long before he proved to her that he was an expert in the kitchen.

Her mother often told them that they should have a cooking reality TV show. It was a very rare compliment coming from her mother, but Phyllis wasn't interested in having cameras neither in her face nor in her space. But she had mentioned to Damien several times about publishing a cookbook. Obviously, he had bigger fish to fry because he always changed the subject. They usually cooked together and it was time well spent. For the most part they were partners, friends and lovers. Phyllis had just bought garlic bread and wanted to make sure that he knew about it. There was nothing like dipping savory garlic bread into Damien's homemade tomato pasta sauce.

"I'll be back, girls. You two get along, okay?"

"Okay, mommy," they replied simultaneously without looking up. Usually, Phyllis would clear her throat to make sure they would look at her when she spoke, but she left them alone this time. She was learning to allow them to work things out amongst themselves unlike the way her mother did with her sisters growing up. Any argument or combative behavior was quickly snuffed out by her mother. It was probably why Phyllis had a difficult time getting along with her sisters now. But since Sabrina and Serena were going to be stuck with one another for the rest of their lives, Phyllis decided not to intervene each time they had a dispute.

As she entered the kitchen the familiar aromas and the sight of Damien cooking made her heart swell with pride. Phyllis smiled as she walked up to him. She massaged his broad shoulders tenderly. "Look at my man in here, cooking for his family," Phyllis cooed. "You're really trying to get some tonight, huh?"

Damien chuckled, "Oh, I know that I'm getting all up in that tonight. No doubt about it!" He turned to look at Phyllis dead in the eyes for emphasis. She pulled at his locs and rubbed his back.

"No argument here. It's been too long since we've had the chance to really enjoy each other. Everything has been chaotic since we moved, but it's starting to feel like home."

"Well, tonight, I'm going to enjoy you until I pass out," he confirmed. "I want to christen the living room and our bedroom."

Phyllis chuckled at his big plans to make love to her all over the house as if they were in their twenties again. They probably wouldn't last ten minutes due to exhaustion, but she let him fantasize anyway. She walked to the freezer to pull out the garlic bread. Damien intercepted her path back to the stove and grabbed her by the waist.

"I'm serious, Phyllis. I miss us being together like we used to be," he confessed and nuzzled his forehead onto hers. "Everything can't always be about the house, bills, your family and the twins. We have to make time for us." He kissed her forehead.

"You mean since you've eased up on your gambling? Now you want to spend more time with me? Because last time I checked, I've always been here. Lady Luck is the one who had all of your attention and God knows who else!"

Damien released his hold, snatched the garlic bread from her hand and walked back to the stove. Phyllis regretted spilling her thoughts in that moment because it did feel good having her man express his strong desire for her. It just came out of her mouth. She didn't mean to spoil the moment. But she couldn't help it because it was the truth.

"See? This is the shit that I'm talking about!" He slammed the garlic bread on the counter while he looked for a pan in the cabinets to place it on. "Things go from sugar to shit real quick with you. I'm trying to have a moment with you, but nooooo... you want to bring up my issues. Damn! How can we move forward when all you do is bring up the past? I told you that I'm working on the gambling. I'm obviously doing better because normally on a Thursday night I would be with..."

All feelings of regret escaped her in that moment. Phyllis cocked her head to the side and folded her arms in front of her chest. "Oh? Do tell. Don't stop now, Damien. Not when you're on a roll."

Phyllis tried to remain calm, but her heart was beating rapidly. Her stomach felt like it dropped to her feet like dead weight. It was all she could do to breathe. She couldn't move as she waited to hear what her husband was going to say next. A fearful thought entered her mind: what if Damien was really cheating on her? Her arrogance had never allowed her to consider that possibility before. Her beauty was undeniable. She was thick in all the right places, handled her business at home, but lately not so much in the bedroom. But still... would he cheat on her? There was no way she could handle a confession of him cheating on her on top of his gambling addiction. But she demanded to know anyway.

"I'm listening!" Phyllis shouted. She was trembling. Her bottom lip gave way as it began to quiver. She blinked her eyes rapidly to fight against to the tears that she refused to let fall down her face.

"Look at you. Just waiting for the other shoe to drop," Damien said disgusted. He shook his head in disbelief and turned the fire down on the stove to a low setting as the sauce simmered. "When did you become like this? It's like you expect the worse from me. Like... like you don't even know me and the love that I have for you."

"You're not answering the question, Damien. You're deflecting and turning things around on me. Just like a guilty person would do!" Phyllis managed to say through the knot in her throat.

"You think that I've been cheating on you?" Damien asked incredulously. "Seriously?"

"What were you about to say? Who do you normally spend your Thursday nights with, Damien?"

Damien rested against the kitchen counter, exhaled and shook his head. Just as he was about to begin speaking, Phyllis's smart phone rang.

"That's you," he announced and turned his attention back to cooking.

Phyllis recognized the ring tone. "It's just my mom. She can wait."

Damien ignored her. As far as he was concerned, he was done with the conversation.

"Damien!" Phyllis shouted. She marched over to him at the stove. Before she could yank his arm he quickly turned around. Sometimes Phyllis would allow her emotions to get out of control and become physical with Damien.

"Be cool, Phyllis," he demanded. He put his hand up to create space between them. It was all he could to keep her off of him.

The phone rang again.

"You better answer that." Damien advised with his eyebrows raised.

Phyllis mashed her lips together and stormed off. As she entered her bedroom to retrieve her phone from her purse, it rang again. Same ring tone. It was her mother, again. Phyllis wondered what in the world could be so urgent.

"Dag, mama! Who died?" Phyllis asked, annoyed that she was being interrupted just when she was about to get Damien to confess.

Another moment of regret came over her when she heard her mother crying. Phyllis sat on the bed and hunched over. "I'm so sorry, mama. I'm on my way."

She hung up the phone and sobbed. A deep, loud moan followed. Too much was happening at the same time, in the same night. Phyllis felt helpless and out of control. She didn't know what to do.

Damien came into their bedroom and sat next to her. The twins stood in the hallway holding hands. None of them had ever heard such a noise come from Phyllis.

"Babe, what's wrong?" Damien asked, concerned that something happened to her mother. "What happened?"

"It's Colette, and the kids," Phyllis sobbed. "There was a fire."

11

Dawn

There was nothing Dawn could do or say to change Vine's mind. It was over. The night he caught Kara between Dawn's legs was enough for him. Dawn explained desperately that Kara had drugged her and forced herself on her, but Vine wasn't convinced. Kara's smug expression on her face certainly didn't improve matters either. Vine had raised his voice in a manner that Dawn had never heard before. She was actually frightened about what he would do to her and Kara. He had all but pushed Kara out the door, called her all types of filthy names and warned her to never come back.

Dawn sat stiff on the bed when Vine entered the room. She cried trying to explain what took place the best way she could considering that she was drunk and drugged, but Vine told her to shut her mouth. He grabbed her by the shoulders and shook her as hard as he could.

"What's the matter with you, huh?" His voice strained, holding a tight grip on her shoulders. They were eye to eye. Tears streamed out of hers and fury burned in his. "I'm not enough for you? Is that it? I've put up with your recreational drugs, your drinking, your flirting with other men right in front of me, your secret text messages, your unexplained absence, but this... Being with another woman, takes the cake!"

"I swear, babe, I was trying to fight her off, but she drugged me," Dawn sobbed. She lowered her head in shame.

"I didn't see you fighting her off at all," Vine replied, letting her go with a shove. "I fucking love you, Dawn. How could you do this to me? To us?"

"I love you too," Dawn cried, reaching for him, but he snatched away from her.

"Just shut up!" Vine shouted, leaving the room. He paced the living room and kitchen, occasionally punching the wall. Dawn had never seen Vine in a violent, angry rage.

She begged for Vine to believe her and even that was out of character for Dawn. She was desperate. Why couldn't he see that she was telling the truth? If Dawn didn't know any better, she would think that he was looking for an out and this was the perfect escape. She truly loved Vine, but it didn't seem to matter to him. All that mattered was he caught her in the act. An act to which she was not a willing participant. Vine had convinced himself that she cheated on him with a woman. Dawn could tell that his pride was hurt. He had been sleeping on the sofa, although it was uncomfortable, he told Dawn that it was better than being in the bed with a confused, dishonest woman.

After a few days of pleading for Vine's forgiveness and understanding, Dawn finally found her pride again. She went on go-sees for magazine shoots just to occupy her time and thoughts. They had been living in silence ever since, only speaking when necessary. It was killing Dawn inside. Practicing silence was foreign to her. She refused to confide in anyone about what happened. She certainly was not the type to put all of her business on social media either. If things didn't improve before she left for Chicago, she decided to definitely confide in her mother, among other things.

After she returned from Chicago for the holidays, she was sure that things would return to normal. They probably needed this break from each other, Dawn concluded. But she still had hoped Vine would use his ticket to come home for Thanksgiving as well. He seemed to be in a good mood, watching a reality TV show that came on right before *"The Haves and Have Nots"*. Lately, he had been immersing himself in every episode to familiarize himself with the cast and the roles they played on the show. Dawn thought asking him about Chicago before the show aired would be the best time.

She looked in the mirror on their bedroom wall, pinched her nipples so they could harden and be erect enough to be seen through her tank top. Then she sucked her bottom lip to make it plump - a trick she learned along the way in the modeling industry - applied lip gloss, fluffed her wild, curly hair and walked slowly up to him as he sat on the sofa. As she walked past him, she touched his shoulder. Vine cringed. Dawn exhaled disappointed by his reaction. It wasn't quite the response that she was expecting. But she took a seat a few inches away from him on the sofa anyway. She sat up straight, with a slight arch in her back and sucked up her feelings.

"Vine, I just want to know if you still plan on going home for Thanksgiving next week," she said searching his face. His eyes were still fixated on the television. She could tell that he wasn't really paying attention, but rather purposely not acknowledging her presence. Vine ignoring her was driving her insane, and he knew it. He was actually good at it too. Dawn thought about rephrasing the question so it wouldn't seem so selfish. It sounded like it was all about her desires, and no consideration for his. "Would you still feel comfortable seeing me and my family during the holidays if you decide to come to Chicago?"

"You see this right here?" Vine snapped, finally looking at Dawn, but pointing to the television commercial featuring the Tyler Perry show. "That's the only thing I'm concerned about next week. Going to Atlanta to make an impression on the man who can change my whole life for the better as an actor, that's all. I can use my ticket to visit my family in Chicago any time. We don't need to be in the same city at the same time. We don't even need to be in the space at the same time... anymore."

"Wait, what?" Dawn was not expecting that reply. She felt her cheeks flush with embarrassment. Usually, she always had inklings when a man had lost interest in their relationship which gave her the opportunity to end things first. But surely, Vine wasn't officially breaking up with her. "I... I just think we need some time apart. When I get back from Chicago..."

"I don't *want* you to come back, Dawn," Vine admitted harshly. It wasn't so much that he had said these words, allowed them to slip out of his mouth and fill the air that bothered Dawn. No. It was how he said it with such disdain for her that caused her stomach to turn and blood to rush like fire through her body.

Dawn inhaled and exhaled repeatedly. She clenched her teeth together so hard that her temples began to throb. "So you mean to tell me, that you're going to throw away three years over somebody like Kara!"

"No!" Vine shouted, rising to his feet. "YOU have thrown away three years over somebody like Kara!"

"What's this really about, Vine?" Dawn probed. "It seems like you're looking for an excuse to be done with me. Before you left the house that day you were in your feelings about something. You never replied to my text message when I asked what was bothering you... Or so I thought you didn't reply. But still..."

"I *did* reply to your text message. Your lesbian friend put your phone on airplane mode, remember?" Vine countered.

Dawn had later found out that her smartphone was on airplane mode apparently for hours when she was with Kara. She certainly had not put her phone on that mode so the only explanation was Kara did it when Dawn went to the restroom at the bar. Dawn had not only missed Vine's text messages, but also a text from her mother and sister, Phyllis, about Colette having a fire in her apartment. It wasn't until she checked Facebook that she found out about the fire.

She was getting chewed out from all fronts over spending one evening with Kara. Lately, she had been apologizing to everyone, although it really wasn't her fault. She was getting sick of explaining herself. Dawn had to explain to her family that her phone was "accidentally" placed on airplane mode and that's why she didn't respond right away. They understood her mishap, but she couldn't say the same for Vine. He just wouldn't let it go.

He pointed the remote at the television to turn it off and then tossed it on the sofa. Dawn hoped that this gesture meant that he was finally ready to communicate. She decided to soften her tone, hoping it would smooth things over if only a little bit.

"Yes, you did text back, eventually, but I didn't see Kara until almost two hours after our initial text. You chose not to respond to me then, and you're not responding now. I've apologized and I don't even know why. Hell, I'm the one who was drugged and almost raped by a woman! I thought was she was my friend. And now I'm losing my best friend, my man, my lover over it?"

Vine grunted, shoved his hands in his pants pockets and stared at Dawn for a while before speaking. She had a good point.

"You still don't know what bothered me that day?" Vine probed.

Dawn shook her head, wiping her nose before her emotions escaped.

"Look, Dawn, I love what I do at the café. It takes skill and talent to become a barista. You've never appreciated my craft. You've never supported me about something that I love to do when it comes to the café."

"I do support you..."

"Yes, you do when it comes to my craft in acting. I'm a good actor, but there's more to me than acting. It was my craft at the café that caught the attention of the casting director. I actually have a backup plan to open up a café of my own just in case this acting career doesn't take off or suddenly ends quickly. "

"You've never shared that with me," Dawn replied offended.

"Why would I? You show no interest in that area of my life. That's what I meant that day, you just don't get it. I need a woman in my life that will support what I love. I need someone with similar interests. I'm looking for wife material. But you... you're only interested in things that involve you somehow. Anything outside of that you make a mockery of it. And that right there, Dawn, is the definition of a selfish person."

"Well, excuse the hell outta me then," Dawn replied, throwing her hands in the air. "I had no idea making coffee was so important to you!"

Vine folded his arms across his chest and shrugged, "You just proved my point."

The silence between them was deafening. Dawn was on the defense, but didn't have a comeback. She ran her fingers through her curls and nodded in defeat. Her bottom lip was going to be raw by the time this conversation was done. If she wasn't gnawing at it, she was biting it to stop it from quivering.

"So, if you've felt this way about me all along, then why three years? Why have me move all the way to New York? Why did you stay this long with me?"

"I'd be lying if I said that I didn't love you, because I do love you, Dawn. But I didn't ask you to move here. You wanted to advance your modeling career and you thought New York would be good for you too, remember?"

Dawn nodded. He was right. That's the way it went. She jumped at the chance to move to New York to be in the spotlight. New York seemed like the place to rub elbows, be seen, get discovered, and mix with the celebrities who mattered. She wasn't going to deny that.

Sitting on the arm of the sofa, Vine continued, "Dawn, let's be honest. I was never going to be enough for you. I've never once cheated on you. I had everything that I needed right here. Yes, even though you are a selfish, self-centered person. You were enough for me, but you seem to like a lot of attention from all types of people. Men *and* women alike. I work in a café where people come to sober up after a wild night of partying, after the theater, or even a fashion show. People talk, Dawn. New York is a small city. You've made quite a name for yourself, too. You're even one of the hottest models on Instagram. I just never knew that you would do whatever it takes to get to the top."

Dawn was completely caught off guard. It had never occurred to her that Vine might have heard gossip about her at the café. The lifestyle that she led outside of their apartment, the one she had hoped Vine never knew about, he had known all along. She hung her head in shame.

"I haven't known you or your family that long, but I do know that you weren't raised like that. The pics you post on the Gram don't leave anything to the imagination. Unless you're trying to be the next Playboy bunny or pin-up for Maxim magazine, I don't see the purpose. The drugs, the excessive drinking, sleeping around with..." Vine couldn't complete his sentence. He got up to pace the floor, searching her face a few times. He exhaled and shook his head. "I've tried my best to look past it, but this mess with Kara took the cake."

"Okay then," Dawn conceded. "This weekend I'll pack as much as I can on the flight to Chicago, and I'll send for the rest of my things after the holidays. After that, I'll be out of your life for good, since that's the way you want it."

"Don't worry about it. I can do that for you," Vine replied. "Just leave a forwarding address. I'll take care of it."

Dawn scoffed in disbelief.

Vine grabbed his coat and scarf in a swift fashion and left their apartment without another word. She watched what seemed in slow motion as the man she loved walked out of the door with finality. Dawn bent her knees to her chest and held on tight as if they would run away at any second. How could the man that she fell in love with be ready to end things so easily? She moved out of town for him, and yes, for her goals too. But she cooked, cleaned, cheered him on, and actually made love to him, repeatedly. Not fucking, but actually making love to a man. Vine was her first experience with making love. Dawn had broken all of her rules for him.

Vine was right, she was a mess, but she wasn't willing to apologize for it. Dawn was convinced that she was a beautiful ball of chaos and that's what made her special. Nobody was going to make her feel bad about that. Nobody.

12

Jonetta

Carpeting would be nice instead of the hardwood floors in Georgia's house. Jonetta was growing tired of her grandchildren already these past two days. They were ripping and running through the house all the time. She would have them go to the basement to play, but there was way too much furniture and other things down there that the children could possibly damage. Instead, she tried sitting them down to color, read, sing, anything but run across the hardwood floors making all types of noise. That only lasted a few minutes before one of them was on their feet again. But what else was she going to do with them? Certainly they couldn't go with their father. Colette would try to kill Owen if she knew that he had her children anywhere near his side-piece, Shante. Although he had time on his hands since he was not working, Jonetta didn't trust him to care for his children like she could. Especially not Delilah, being a baby and all. She had gotten so big and plump over the past few weeks and also very demanding. Jonetta knew how to care for her grandchildren just fine.

The doctor was supposed to give an update yesterday on Colette, but no progress had been made. If Jonetta didn't know any better, she would swear that Colette was milking this hospital stay for everything just to get a break from her life. But that wasn't her style. That was more along the antics Phyllis would try. Colette adored her children, unruly and all. Jonetta knew that if it were up to her, she'd be right there with them spoiling them, and making sure that they were alright. It was just taking more time for her to be released from the hospital than she had thought. Smoke inhalation was serious and it didn't help that Colette was hysterical. The doctors needed to do whatever they could for Colette to get better. If that meant a longer hospital stay, then Jonetta was fine with it. She would just need to be a little more creative with activities for her grandchildren.

Jonetta admitted that her daughters were nothing like her when it came to parenting. If you asked her, they paid way too much attention to their children. Always monitoring them, letting them have their say, and being present in adult conversations. This was a new generation of mothers indeed, but Jonetta just kept her distance as much as she could so she wouldn't offend anyone with her true thoughts.

"Cornell!" Jonetta called out to her only grandson. "Come here!"

Cornell, the spitting image of his father, came running down the hallway. Jonetta frowned at him. He looked wide-eyed, "Yes, gram-gram?"

"Listen, you're the oldest, right?"

Cornell nodded trying to catch his breath.

"Gram-gram needs you to play follow the leader with your sisters. I want you to slow down with the running, and play a game in a circle. But not duck-duck-goose. Do you understand me?"

"Yes, gram-gram," Cornell chuckled. "I have a game we can play. But we're hungry too! Can we go..."

"No, we cannot go anywhere. But I can make lunch for you. Now go on and do as you're told."

"Okay," Cornell obeyed, walking very slowly down the hall.

Jonetta shook her head, reached for her pack of cigarettes and sighed realizing that she was all out. "This is what happens when I'm not in my routine." She grunted angrily. Although she kept saying that she was going to quit smoking, today was not the day.

The baby monitor lights were flickering and she heard Delilah making a noise. Phyllis had bought the monitor set so Jonetta wouldn't have to run up and down the stairs to see after Delilah while she stayed with her. The noise faded and Jonetta exhaled, grateful that she wasn't about to start crying or having one of her fits that she's been having these past two days. Phyllis brought some of Colette's clothes to place near the baby for a familiar scent, but that wasn't working either. Delilah was a smart baby; she wanted to see her mommy's face.

Phyllis had offered to spend the night or switch days with her mother to help care for the children, but Jonetta declined. Now she regretted that decision as she made turkey sandwiches. They would have to do until she could go grocery shopping for the items her grandchildren liked. Junk mostly. But for now someone would have to go the store for her to get cigarettes before her nerves wreaked havoc.

As she reached for her smartphone, it rang and an unsaved number displayed. Against her better judgment, Jonetta answered.

"Mrs. Miller speaking."

"Just the person that I'm looking for," a man's voice with a thick accent replied.

Jonetta rolled her eyes. Of all people, she was not in the mood for his nonsense.

"How did you get my number?" Jonetta snapped. "What do you want from me?"

"I'm resourceful," Big Louie replied, sounding so pleased with himself. She could imagine the huge smile that came across his face. "All I need is your signature."

"My signature, for what?"

"To sign over the house to me," he answered her question as if it were obvious. "I have everything drawn up and ready for you to sign."

Jonetta shook her head. The sins of her past were catching up with her. She needed it to go away and fast.

13

Colette

Colette blinked rapidly as she opened her eyes to more bright lights and a beeping sound. She raised her hands in the air until she could see them. A chill came over her and goose bumps rose on her arms instantly. Her right arm had an IV in it and her eyes followed the tubes up to the bag dangling almost directly above her head. Her heart monitor began to beep rapidly. Fear struck her as she recalled the last time she was here it was because Owen had hit her so hard that she blacked out. She feared that was the reason she was here now.

"Help," she whispered. Her eyes welled up with tears as her eyes darted around the room. It was evident that she was in a hospital, but she didn't know why. She cleared her throat and tried again, "Help!"

A plump, white nurse and her sister, Phyllis, came rushing into her room.

"You're awake!" Phyllis exclaimed. She smiled and clasped her hands together.

Colette blinked her eyes a few times trying to focus on her sister. Phyllis's hair was twisted up in such a fashion that Colette could not stop staring. It appeared to be locs with streaks of gold. Colette wondered

102

had she been in the hospital long enough for Phyllis to lock her hair? She studied her sister's face. Her light brown eyes were filled with relief. For the first time Colette felt genuinely loved by her sister. Colette reached for her sister's hand and held it tightly.

The nurse was breathing heavily just from that short dash from the hallway to her bedside. As she checked her vitals she smiled at Colette revealing her cigarette and coffee stained teeth.

"Try taking deep breaths, Mrs. Aldridge," she said softly and patted her hand. "Welcome back."

"Why..." Colette touched her neck while she cleared her throat. It was scratchy and dry. "Why am I here? Where are my children?"

"Here's some water," Phyllis offered. She poured ice water from the pitcher that was on a tray and plopped a straw in it.

Colette turned her head refusing to drink until she had answers. She vaguely remembered hearing sirens, but her memory was too cloudy. Water certainly was not going to help bring it back.

"Mrs. Aldridge, there was a fire in your apartment a few days ago," the nurse began to explain. "You and your children all escaped, and they are doing just fine."

"They're perfectly fine and staying with mama until you get better," Phyllis reassured her. "Here, drink this."

Colette leaned her head towards the straw and took a sip. Tears began to well up in her eyes thinking about her children. She closed her eyes and sighed. "Running, yelling and smoke," she said as a tear rolled down her cheek. Phyllis patted her knee to console her. The nurse announced that she was going to inform the doctor that she was awake and alert. As soon as the nurse closed the door behind her Phyllis sat on the stool next to her bed and slid in closer.

"How did the fire start in the kitchen?" Phyllis asked.

Colette rubbed her forehead trying to remember, but she couldn't. "How long have I been in the hospital?"

"For two days," Phyllis replied. "You were heavily sedated. They said that you were hysterical and collapsed right outside when you saw them bring out Lydia. She's doing just fine though. It was only a little smoke inhalation that caused her to faint. Nothing major, but the way you reacted must have sent you into some sort of shock. We thought that you would wake up the next morning, but you never did. Girl, you gave us all a good scare. Mama came by with the kids yesterday, but you were still asleep. So instead, she went on another floor to visit Fred with Georgia. He's a permanent resident now until they can move him to a hospice facility. I think mama is just about sick of seeing the inside of this hospital. But, of course, being the social butterfly she is, everybody knows her name."

"Only two days?" Colette questioned. "Then how did you lock your hair like that so fast?"

Caught off guard Phyllis blushed and touched her hair self-consciously. "Oh, these are faux locs. But enough about me. They said your neighbor Mr. Green helped you escape the fire. He was treated and released though. You, on the other hand, are still here and I've come to bust you outta here!"

"The fire," Colette said softly and moaned. She pressed her head deeper into the light weight hospital pillow, closed her eyes and sighed. Bits and pieces were popping into her mind now that she was fully awake. She remembered coughing, running to grab Delilah...

"My baby!" Colette shot straight up in a panic. "Where's Delilah? Who has my baby? I never saw her again once I came outside!"

Phyllis sighed, "Didn't I just tell you that all of your kids are fine? She's with mama too. Please lie back and calm down. We don't want them putting you on the psych ward. They were already asking us if you should be on suicide watch, if you were pregnant, were you on any prescription medications, if you had any heart disease, among other things. They were asking us a ton of questions. And of course, we couldn't get in touch with Owen to really confirm anything." Phyllis rolled her eyes and shook her head.

Colette frowned and shook her head. She was distraught, not crazy. She was not on any drugs, prescribed or otherwise. But she was pregnant. This news wouldn't be welcomed, especially since she had lied to her mother about having her tubes tied after giving birth to Delilah.

She decided to keep it to herself for now. Soon enough everyone would see that she was expecting her fifth child with her husband, the man everyone seemed to hate with a passion. Wearily she rubbed her forehead.

"Listen," Phyllis leaned in closer to her sister. "Even if you do remember how it happened just keep it to yourself for insurance purposes, ya know? Don't admit any fault when you talk to your landlord or anybody for that matter. The way you've been doped up anybody would believe that you just don't remember. Keep it that way so you can get some settlement money."

"I honestly can't jog my memory right now," Colette replied a bit irritated by her sister's advice. Phyllis was always coming up with ways on how to get over on somebody. She was always like that growing up too, never taking ownership or responsibility for her actions. Any issues that occurred were always everyone's fault, but hers. Things seemed to work in her favor when she really wanted to scheme her way out of a mess. Sometimes Colette wished she had those types of smarts, but then again her mother always warned her about karma.

"I just want to see my kids. Can you call mama for me?"

"Don't worry, girl, the fire department has the full report anyway," Phyllis replied and reached into her purse for her smartphone. "I'll text mama the good news that you're awake, but it's too late for visiting hours especially with children."

It was nearly seven in the evening and visiting hours would be over in an hour. It would be impossible for their mother to prepare the children and get them there before visiting hours would be over.

"But they're *my* children and I want to see them," Colette insisted.

Phyllis raised her eyebrow and pursed her lips, but before she could respond the doctor knocked at the door and entered. He towered over Colette and immediately began to go over her stats without introducing himself. He barely looked up from the chart on the clipboard. His thick Middle Eastern accent combined all syllables that it sounded like run on sentences, one after another.

Phyllis cleared her throat and the doctor finally looked up. His dark eyes looked fatigued, like he had been on shift for 72 hours straight.

Although he was handsome, he had no bed side manners at all. The doctor continued with his prognosis prescribing sleep medication and muscle relaxers, if needed. Finally the doctor looked at Colette, flashed a half smile, and told her she would be released in the morning.

Georgia drove Colette to her house where her children were staying with Jonetta. Since she was always at the hospital by Fred's side, she offered to take her instead of having Jonetta round up the children. Colette welcomed the company of her aunt Georgia. She was always so peaceful.

"You look much better now that you've gotten some rest," Georgia said and glanced in Colette's direction. "Yes, you look well rested. I know it must be so frustrating at times handling all the children. But you have to learn how to lean on your family for help."

Colette studied her aunt's face. It was aged but gracefully with every wrinkle in the right spot. Her salt and pepper hair framed her round face and complimented her light brown eyes. The wrinkles in her hand smoothed out with every turn of the wheel. She was always dressed nicely and today was no exception.

"I know," Colette finally responded. "But as mama always says, 'it's my bed and I have to lie in it'. I just don't want to burden any-one. Everybody's plate is full. My little ones can really be rambunctious sometimes."

"Weren't we all as kids?" Georgia laughed. "Your children are no different than any other normal kids. They are welcome in my home. You all are welcome in my home as long as you like. As you know my new home is at the hospital beside Fred's side until... Well, until the Lord sees fit to do what needs to be done."

"That's awfully nice of you," Colette smiled. "I'm sorry about Uncle Fred, too."

Georgia's eyes glazed over and she swallowed hard over the lump in her throat. "The Lord's will be done, not mine. If it were up to me, I'd take his ornery ass home today!"

They shared a laughed. That was the first time Colette had heard her aunt use a curse word. It was even more shocking that she used it to describe her beloved Fred. After being together for decades Colette figured a few adjectives to describe her husband was befitting. Colette had more than a few to describe Owen and none were as gentle as 'ass'.

"But he'll be going to hospice care," Georgia continued. "It's just his time, sugar. We were all born to die."

A thought struck Colette. "Has anyone reached Owen? Did he even come to the hospital?" Colette searched her aunt's face.

Georgia frowned and shook her head. "Sorry, sugar."

"Has anyone been by my apartment to see the damage?" Colette asked changing the subject. "I need to check with my landlord to see when or *if* we can move back in. I have to go there to get whatever is left. If there is anything left worth keeping."

Colette sighed and stared out the window. The chore ahead of her already overwhelmed her before it even began. Just the thought of having a conversation with her landlord made her cringe. He was not the most pleasant person even when they were on time with the rent. In that moment she wished Owen was there to handle everything.

"Your mother went by, but she didn't say much about the damage," Georgia replied. "She just went to gather what she could for children and some of your clothes. That's all I know. Would you like me to swing by now?"

"No," Colette replied quickly. She shook her head. "I would rather see my children first. A moment of joy, then the pain of everything else."

14

Phyllis

She sat naked on her bed taking deep breaths. Damien had just reminded her of how much he loved and missed her. Completely exhausted from the eventful past few days with Colette, the kids, getting them things they needed at Georgia's house, all she wanted was sleep, but her husband wanted her. And since Damien sincerely swore that he wasn't cheating on her - she confirmed it by snooping through his smartphone - she let him have his way with her.

Morning sex was always his favorite. He claimed that it got his day started right. But it did the complete opposite for her. It had been weeks since they made love and Damien had the proof all over her and their sheets. Now she had to clean herself, and do unexpected laundry before it stained the sheets.

Damien was showering in their master bathroom for work. He invited Phyllis to join him, but she refused knowing that it would only turn into another fuck session. Usually that would turn her on, but she was worn out. Phyllis fell backwards and stretched her arms above her head. It felt good to have the whole bed all to herself, even if for a little while. The twins slept with her sometimes when Damien had to work late, or stayed out late gambling. Who knows these days? If it weren't for their bedroom door being locked they would probably try to come in now. But they knew if the door was closed that meant do not disturb mommy and daddy.

The twins were out of school for the holiday and they were being busy bodies. They had half day of school, but Phyllis decided to just keep them home. She listened intently as they chatted amongst themselves. Their footsteps indicated that they were headed to the kitchen. That was Phyllis's cue to get up and get moving before they decide to burn their house down. One fire in the family was enough.

She reached for her purple, waffle weave kimono robe and sighed. Just the thought of everything she had to do today: grocery shopping, running other errands, baking, including keeping the twins busy made her head hurt. The water stopped running in the bathroom and Damien was humming. He was definitely in a good mood and that made Phyllis smile.

He opened the bathroom door singing, "Good Morning. Good Morning, Love." He was not quite the crooner like John Legend, but you couldn't tell Damien that. His legs were spread apart, towel wrapped around his waist, body oiled, and his cologne slowly filled the air. Damien smiled showing all of his pearly whites. He was feeling good. Phyllis made a mental note to give him a quickie on Thanksgiving morning so he could be in the same mood.

"I'm going to get breakfast started," Phyllis said. She snatched the sheets off the mattress swiftly before he got any bright ideas about round two.

"Come here, girl," Damien cooed, licking his lips.

Phyllis hesitated. While he was feeling squeaky clean, she had yet to even wipe herself off. She smirked at him while he motioned for her to come to him. She obliged and walked towards him with the sheets in her hands. He lifted her chin and kissed her softly.

"Do you mind if I get in here for a moment to clean off?"

"Not at all," Damien replied, stepping aside so she could enter their bathroom. "Can I watch?"

Phyllis pursed her lips and handed him the sheets. "Toss those in the wash," she instructed and closed the bathroom door behind her. She grabbed a towel from the bar on the wall, ran warm water and wiped between her thighs. A sigh of relief escaped her lips. The warmth felt good. A nice soak in the tub would've been nice, but her motherly duties called.

When she opened the bathroom door, Damien was still humming, but to another tune this time. Phyllis recognized it as D'Angelo's, "Really Love". He was in full uniform and checking himself out in the mirror. A ponytail was put in place to pull back his sandy brown locs. He popped his collar, feeling himself. Phyllis couldn't help but laugh. It was a pleasure seeing her husband in a good mood, but his humming was way off key.

"Let me go before the girls decide to cook," Phyllis said, reminding him that they were awake. "And don't forget to toss those in the wash." She reminded him pointing at the sheets he put on the floor by the foot of their bed.

"Okay," Damien replied, slapping her on her plump butt as she walked past. "But I don't have time to sit down to eat. So can you make scrambled eggs on toast for me?"

"Sure," she replied.

Phyllis grabbed her smartphone from the dresser and put it in her robe pocket. She walked down the hallway to the kitchen and found the twins had made a mess with cereal. Their bowls overflowed with milk and cereal was all over the counter and floor. Phyllis knew they were up to something. But she couldn't necessarily blame them because it was no telling how long she and Damien were going to take with their morning lovemaking session.

"Morning, mommy," Serena said sheepishly. She scooped a spoonful of cereal in her mouth while keeping her eyes on Phyllis.

"Mmm hmm. Good morning girls," Phyllis replied. Shaking her head she handed Sabrina paper towels to clean up the mess. "You just couldn't wait, huh? I was about to cook breakfast, but since you decided on cereal, you have to eat that."

"Sorry, mommy," Sabrina whined.

"Just clean it up, sweetie," Phyllis said softly. She didn't want to start the morning out fussing. It was the holidays after all.

As she pulled the string on the kitchen window blinds, the sunlight poured in brightening the whole kitchen. A car rode past thumping loud music and Phyllis rolled her eyes. She hated that her kitchen window faced the street, but it did give her a bird's eye view of everything happening on the block. She opened the closet door to get the broom and began sweeping up the cereal.

On top of the refrigerator she heard a buzzing sound. It was her wireless Bluetooth headset. She hid it up there from the twins because Damien had bought an expensive kind. As she reached for them she decided against answering. It was too early in the morning to hold a conversation with anyone, as far as she was concerned. On second thought, she wrapped them around her neck instead.

Damien exhaled. "I'll just pick something up on my way," he said when he entered the kitchen. He was clearly disappointed that his breakfast had not been prepared yet.

"Hi daddy!" The twins ran over to give him a huge hug.

"Morning girls," Damien replied, bending down to hug them both. They returned to the table to finish eating their huge bowls of cereal.

"It won't take long to scramble some eggs and make toast, Damien," Phyllis said, trying to reason with him. "You see the mess that I walked into! Just give me a minute."

"It's cool, babe. I gotta run." He walked over to kiss Phyllis. "Girls, be good and listen to your mom. When I get home I want to see those famous oatmeal chocolate chip cookies on a platter waiting for me."

"Okay, daddy," they both replied.

Phyllis pursed her lips and cocked her head to the side. That meant more work for her, but clearly that didn't register with Damien. Before she could say anything, he was out the door. He left for work earlier than usual since it was holidays and deliveries were in abundance. Phyllis didn't mind his long hours because it meant more money in his check. That's one thing they could never have too much of these days.

Phyllis swept up the last crumbs of the cereal and dumped them in the garbage when her wireless set buzzed again. She glanced at her phone in her pocket and saw Dawn's face on the screen. She put one ear bud in her ear and clicked the button to answer.

"Hey sis!" Phyllis exclaimed. She was sorry that she hadn't answered the phone earlier.

"Hi, Phyllis! Glad you answered this time," Dawn said. "Guess who's on her way home?"

"What time do you land?"

"Around two-thirty and mom is picking me up from Midway. I'm at JFK airport now just waiting to board. We have to make one stop in Atlanta then head to Chicago."

"Well, I probably won't get a chance to see you today, but definitely tomorrow. You know we have to do all of the major cooking at Aunt Georgia's so mama can have a watchful eye on us. But I'm going to do some baking today with the twins." Phyllis glanced over at the twins and they were beaming.

"I can't wait to see everyone and hangout with my sisters."

"I know me too. We definitely have to go out before you leave on Saturday. Maybe after Thanksgiving dinner we can sneak out for a bit. There's a lot do on that night. I have a few invites and events in my time-line on Facebook. We can check one of them out that night."

"Right..." Dawn's voice trailed off.

Phyllis frowned. "You do wanna kick it, don't you?"

"Of course I do!" Dawn said. "We're going to make it happen, trust me."

"I'll see you tomorrow girl, but text me when you land, okay?"

"Will do," Dawn agreed. "See you soon!"

They ended the call.

Phyllis sent a group text to Colette and her mother to let them know that Dawn was at the airport and would be arriving in the afternoon. She sent a separate text directly to Colette:

Phyllis: *Hope you're feeling better and settled in at Aunt Georgia's.*
Colette: *Slowly getting there. Not in the holiday spirit.*
Phyllis: *Well, get your shit together. Dawn is coming home and wants to kick it with us.*
Colette: *Don't have much shit to get together! It's all burnt up remember?*
Phyllis: *Start with your attitude and the rest will fall into place!*
Colette: *Oh, gee, thanks! I'll get right on it. Nothing like good, sisterly advice.*

After that last response, Phyllis rolled her eyes and put the phone back into her pocket. She didn't have time to go back and forth with Colette today. All she knew was Colette had better be ready to hang out when they were ready.

Phyllis walked back to her bedroom to change clothes. Upon entering she saw the sheets were still on the floor. Now she was glad that she didn't cook Damien any breakfast like he asked since he couldn't do anything she asked. He could forget about the cookies and morning quickie on Thanksgiving morning. As far as she was concerned, they were even.

15

Dawn

After being at the airport for over an hour, Dawn had finally given up on looking for Vine to arrive at the gate. He had a carry-on suitcase sitting at the front door, but she had not seen him that morning. She, on the other hand, had packed a large suitcase with all of her essential items, shoes, and coats included. As a reminder of her presence, Dawn purposely left behind the fan on the dresser that she used for night sweats. Knowing Vine, he would probably toss it out when he returned.

Frustrated that he wanted to end things on a sour note, Dawn decided to write a short note expressing her feelings. She placed it on top of his suitcase before leaving and gently closed the door to her place of residence for the past three years behind her.

It still stung that it was over between them. It was unbelievable, but Vine's absence and silence as of late made it quite believable. Dawn was sad. It was an unfamiliar emotion. Very rarely did she experience sadness. She always did what pleased her. Even when she wasn't chosen for a modeling gig, sadness didn't overwhelm her because she saw it as an opportunity to do something else with her time. But this, a harsh unexpected breakup with Vine, crushed her. He didn't even so much as say good-bye or give her a hug. If she only saw it coming Dawn could've been more prepared to deal with her feelings.

She sulked staring out of the window, watching the planes land and take off. It was pretty much metaphoric of her life. A lot of take offs and lots of landings, but Dawn always landed on her feet. Sharply, she inhaled. A drink would do her nerves some good. She decided to grab a drink from the airport bar across the busy pedway from her terminal. She barely made eye contact with the bartender or any of the patrons. After she ordered a glass of Cabernet Sauvignon an older black man in a suit with salt and pepper gray hair, offered his seat at the bar, but she smiled and declined. Dawn figured that he was around her father's age and simply being a gentleman. But this wasn't a time when she felt like being social so she stood at the end of the bar. All she needed was the wine to race through body to relax her mind.

"Nerves, huh?" A man's voice asked from behind her.

Dawn turned around to see Mr. Sugerman staring at her like she was fine chocolate that he was about to devour. She opened her mouth, but no words formed. The bartender placed a wine glass in front of her, emptying the entire six ounce wine bottle.

"Eight dollars," the bartender announced.

Mr. Sugerman handed him a twenty dollar bill and instructed him to keep the change. The bartender thanked him and tended to the other patrons.

"Hi," Dawn said finally. "Thanks for the drink, but you didn't have to..."

"Nonsense," Mr. Sugerman said, flashing a huge smile. He moved in closer and Dawn felt the warmth of his breath right on her nose. And from the smell of things, Mr. Sugerman had already been drinking Scotch.

"Fancy meeting you here after all this time," Mr. Sugerman said, touching Dawn's shoulder. "Heading home for the holidays?"

"Yeah," she answered. Dawn flashed a quick smiled, reached for her glass of wine, took a gulp and glanced around the bar to see if anyone was watching them. Everyone seemed to be tuned into CNN News. They were covering a huge story about the newly released video footage of a white Chicago police officer shooting a black teenaged boy, Laquan McDonald, to death. Dawn wished that she could turn her attention to the news coverage too, but Mr. Sugerman was fixated on her.

"You've ran across my mind a few times since I last saw you," Mr. Sugerman admitted. His eyes examined her from head to toe. He reached to touch her hair. Pleased with how a curl bounced back after he tugged on it, he smiled to himself. He was pawing all over her as if she was a doll and it annoyed Dawn. At that very moment, Mr. Sugerman made her skin crawl.

"Have I?" Dawn asked coyly. She wanted him to just go away so she could enjoy her wine before she boarded the plane. At a loss for words, she took another sip of wine.

"Oh yes, my sweet, pansy. We have some unfinished business that I would like to finish sooner than later," he said, patting her hand and moving in closer. Dawn was pinned between the corner of the bar and Mr. Sugerman blocking her path to exit. The older black man at the bar quickly glanced at them, raised his eyebrows and turned his back. He must've thought she was a prostitute the way Mr. Sugerman was carrying on. It was evident that Mr. Sugerman was old enough to be her great-grandfather. Dawn's cheeks flushed from embarrassment. She cleared her throat, swallowed the last of the wine and pushed the glass away from her.

"I don't think we do, Mr. Sugerman," Dawn replied. She narrowed her eyes, blinking rapidly, hoping that he would get the message.

Mr. Sugerman waved over the bartender and pointed to Dawn's glass, signaling him to give her another round and he ordered a Scotch neat.

"That won't be necessary," Dawn said. "I only wanted one glass of wine. You have a good holiday, Mr. Sugerman."

"Nonsense," Mr. Sugerman replied. "It's the holidays! You should indulge in all the forbidden pleasures. I know I will." He laughed incredulously and stroked the side of her face.

Dawn jerked her head away from him swiftly and grabbed his hand to stop him from continuously petting her. Mr. Sugerman took that opportunity to hold her hand, affectionately rubbing it. He was causing a scene. Dawn scanned the small bar and several patrons had certainly turned their attention in their direction.

"Please, don't do that," she whispered. The traffic in the small bar was growing thicker by the minute. She glanced over to her terminal and did a double take. Her heart felt like it sank to her stomach and someone must've turned up the heat because she broke out into a sweat. It was Vine. He was sitting in the terminal facing her. He quickly looked down at his smartphone and placed his earbuds in both ears.

Dawn gasped and snatched her hand away. "I have to go."

"Hey, pansy, where do you think you're going?" Mr. Sugerman asked slurring his words. He grabbed her elbow firmly. "I just ordered another glass of wine for you. Now, be a lady, drink it and keep me company until it's time for you to board your plane. Or we can go somewhere quieter and ... handle our business."

"Get your fucking hands off of me!" Dawn said loud enough that the all patrons at the bar directed their attention towards them. She snatched away and headed to the first restroom she could find pushing past the busy travelers.

Inside the stall Dawn buried her face inside of her hands breathing heavily. She regretted now not saying those very words the first time she had met Mr. Sugerman. If she had, she wouldn't have been in this current situation. Her mind raced. This was a nightmare. How long had Vine been sitting there? If only she had stayed in her seat, continued watching the planes. But no, she had to go feed her feelings at the bar.

"Fuck!" Dawn yelled, hitting the side of the stall wall.

There was no way that she could talk her way out of this one. It was not hearsay this time. Vine had witnessed it for himself: another man groping on her in public. Dawn could tell him that Mr. Sugerman was just some old guy trying to come on to her. But that lie could only hold depending upon how long Vine had been sitting there watching her. At any time, Vine could've come over to the bar, interrupted them to claim her as his woman, or even rescue her, if nothing else. But that was not Vine's style at all. There was nothing bravado about him, unfortunately.

A lady's voice over the intercom announced that her flight to Chicago was boarding, seating first class passengers. Dawn left the stall and walked to the sink. She looked in the mirror, mashed her lips together, closed her eyes and exhaled. After looking at herself in the mirror, she was disappointed at who she had become since living in New York. She took the hair tie from her wrist, pulled her hair up in a bun, took off her jacket and threw on her shades. That was the best she could do for a disguise from Mr. Sugerman if he was still out there waiting on her.

Another intercom announcement interrupted her rambled thoughts. It was time to go face the music. She walked slowly back to her terminal looking for both Mr. Sugerman and Vine. There was no sign of either of them. She sighed, relieved that she didn't have to face them at that moment. But where did Vine go that fast? Was he headed to Chicago with her after all?

Dawn stood in the line forming for her section. She reached in the side pocket of her purse for her smartphone and decided to call Vine. No answer. She sent him a text. No reply. Her stomach flopped. Feeling rejected made her nauseous and angry at the same time. Her phone alerted that she had a text message. She sucked her teeth when she saw that it was just her mother letting her know that she would be on schedule for picking her up today from Midway airport. After explaining to her mother that she and Vine were taking a break from each other, she offered to get Dawn from the airport so they could have time to talk in peace.

Once on the plane her eyes darted around to see if she could spot Vine. It didn't take long because he was sitting in first class with a window seat. What the hell was he doing in first class? She thought. Dawn booked their seats together on this flight, but he must have upgraded at some point. Vine had put on a baseball cap, pulled it low over his eyes, apparently also wanting to be in disguise. But Dawn recognized that bean head anywhere.

"Vine!" Dawn called out, waving.

Vine looked up, held her gaze but then turned his head to look out the window. Dawn sucked her teeth again. There was nothing that interesting to see out the window, he was blatantly ignoring her. If he wanted her to make a scene on the plane then she was willing to do just that. Once the people in front of her found their seats, she stopped at Vine's row.

"Vine, don't ignore me," Dawn said.

"What do you want, Dawn?" Vine asked, removing an ear bud from his ear.

"We were supposed to sit together on this flight. Why did you up-grade?" That's the only thing Dawn could think of to say. If she could kick herself right then, she would have. There was so much more she wanted to say, could have said, but that's what came out instead.

Vine shook his head and placed the ear bud back in his ear.

"Excuse me," a young Asian lady said. She was standing right behind Dawn looking like a midget who could fit in the overhead suitcase com-partments. "That's my seat." She was pointing to the one next to Vine.

Dawn glanced over her shoulder at the lady and ignored her.

"Vine, I'm sorry," Dawn said.

He ignored her.

Annoyed by that whole situation Dawn decided to keep walking to her seat. She was defeated and it wasn't worth creating an uncomfort-able plane ride for the next three hours. Thankfully, she was only three rows behind Vine and could still see him from where she sat. At the first chance she got, she ordered wine from the flight attendant.

The wine had done its job and Dawn fell into a slumber. She was awakened by someone shaking her arm. It took a minute for Dawn to realize where she was. Her heart was pounding and her head was throb-bing. She rubbed her forehead and turned her attention to the passen-ger next to her.

"Are you alright?" A male passenger asked. His pale face looked flushed and concerned. "Should I ring for the flight attendant?"

Dawn was breathing heavily, but managed to shake her head no. It was just another nightmare, but this time the dark figure was about to turn around to reveal their identity. After she slowed her breathing, Dawn replied, "I'm okay."

"Are you sure? Because…"

"Excuse me," Dawn said, interrupting him. She unbuckled her seatbelt and attempted to get out of her seat. Splashing water on her face would help if she could just get to the restroom.

"Oh, you can't get up now. We're about to land in Atlanta in ten minutes," the man explained.

"Shit!" Dawn replied. "Thanks."

She put her seatbelt back on, looked in Vine's direction and wished that he could come comfort her like always when these nightmares occurred. But they were confined to their seats for now.

The landing was smooth and some passengers clapped for the captain's skill. Once they reached the terminal the unbuckle seat belt sign came on and she saw Vine getting up from his seat. Where was he going? Dawn sat upright in her seat and leaned forward. It was too many people in the aisle for her to make a quick dash to him. For a moment she thought he was coming towards her, but when he reached above for his carryon suitcase, she knew otherwise.

Vine looked in her direction and Dawn threw her hands in the air as if asking him where was he going? In return, Vine threw the peace sign and exited the plane.

16

Jonetta

After doing a final sweep of the kitchen Jonetta lit a cigarette, looked around at her handy work and smiled. Georgia did not keep a tidy home according to Jonetta's standards. She took it upon herself to rearrange furniture and thoroughly clean her sister's house especially since it was almost Thanksgiving. The thought of taking care of two homes frustrated Jonetta and the act of doing it was tiresome.

Big Louie had been persistent about taking her home that formerly belonged to the love of her life to cover all his debts. According to neighbors he had been snooping around the house. He even left a note on the door for Jonetta urging her to call him. But evidently one of those nosey neighbors gave her phone number to him. She was certain that it didn't take much convincing. Big Louie was really slick with words and his accent made any proposition sound that more intriguing.

Now that Colette had moved in with her and Georgia, it was easy for Jonetta to leave the house whenever she felt like it. Her grandchildren were doing well and didn't need her attention as much anymore. She managed to slip out of the house earlier than scheduled without anyone noticing to meet with Big Louie at his church basically to discuss blackmail.

Never too keen on attending church or becoming a faithful member of one, Jonetta was agitated just by being there.

"Isn't this a likely place to meet?" Jonetta remarked when she was finally escorted into Big Louie's office. She looked around in disgust, although his office was kept very well with polished cherry wood furniture, she wanted to let him know that she wasn't pleased about the meeting.

"I figured you might find comfort here among the saints," Big Louie said wryly. He folded his thick hands and placed them on top of his belly. As he leaned back the chocolate leather chair squeaked. Jonetta hoped he would lean back too far and fall on his fat ass, but no dice.

"I will find comfort when you are out of my life for good," Jonetta snapped. "How quickly can we make that happen?"

"Glad you asked," Big Louie said. He reached in his desk drawer and pulled out a blue folder. He opened it in front of Jonetta, allowed her to read over it for a few minutes, then pulled a pin from his suit jacket and handed it to her. "All you have to do is sign right here." He pointed to the blank line where the owner should sign for handing over the deed to the new owner.

Jonetta took the pen from him and read over the document. She placed the pen down on the desk and leaned back. She stared at him thoughtfully for a few minutes in silence.

"Surely, you never mistook me for a fool," she said finally.

"Not at all," Big Louie replied, leaning forward with innocent eyes.

"Then what do I get out of signing over the deed to you for a dollar?" She quipped. "Oh, yes, I can read too!"

"What do you get? You get peace in your life. You get me out of your pretty hair. You get to go on with your lies... I mean life," Big Louie remarked and chuckled, pleased with himself. "Just consider this for a moment, Johnnie. If you put the house on the market, you would have to fix it up, and that means putting money into something that you don't even want. Not only that, it would take time and the rest of your time you have here on Earth should be spent with your loving family. Wouldn't you agree?"

"You're one sick, twisted mother fuc -"

"Now, now Johnnie, there's no place in the house of the Lord for that type of talk," he chided. "I actually thought you would agree to these terms. But if not..." he reached across his desk to grab the paperwork, but Jonetta snatched it before he could touch it.

"If this means once and for all getting you out of my life, then so be it," Jonetta fumed. "And now that I mentioned it, I don't see a clause in here stating such. Write that in somewhere on this document and I'll sign immediately."

Big Louie tapped his fingers together and stared at Jonetta. He sucked his teeth and reached towards the phone to call in his secretary. He mumbled for her to come into his office and hung up the phone. Within seconds the young twenty-something came strutting in the office. The light beamed off her shiny chocolate legs as she walked in a tight gray pencil skirt. She wasn't wearing any pantyhose in the middle of November. And she probably didn't have any panties on either, Jonetta thought. The suit jacket that she was wearing when Jonetta first arrived apparently had been left at her desk so she could show off her muscular arms and perky boobs in a silk, pink camisole.

"Yes, Pastor Paul," she cooed, slinging her extra-long wavy weave over her shoulder. Even her shoulder was glistening. What did this heifer do? Dowse herself with Crisco? Jonetta wondered.

Big Louie was writing on a notecard and handed it to her when he was done. "I need you to add this sentence in the document after this paragraph," he pointed at the paper showing the secretary where he wanted it. She leaned in and her camisole loosely draped from her chest revealing that she wasn't wearing a bra. Big Louie did a double-take, tried to keep his composure and shifted in his seat.

Jonetta grunted and shook her head. Typical, she thought.

"I'll be right back, Pastor," she said and bounced out of the office, closing the door behind her.

"You could've written it in and it still would have held up in a court of law, you know," Jonetta remarked.

"I know, but I'd rather have things done in decency and in order," Big Louie countered.

"Decency? You don't even know the definition of decency. You're running a whore house guised as a church. It's the same thing you'll do with the house, I'm sure. Is that why you want it so bad?"

"Actually, I've decided to turn the house into a shelter for women and children," Big Louie announced proudly.

"Well, wonders never cease," Jonetta replied, sitting back in her chair. "Starting them out young, huh?"

Before he could respond the all but too eager secretary returned with the revised document. "All done, Pastor Paul," she handed over the document with a wide grin.

"Ah, perfect timing. You're the best I've ever had, Alyssa," Big Louie purred.

"In more ways than one, I'm sure," Jonetta mumbled.

The secretary shot her a look and exited quietly.

"If this suits your approval, please sign it," Big Louie suggested, handing Jonetta the pen again.

Jonetta read it, signed it and excused herself.

"Wait a minute," Big Louie said, rising from his chair slowly. "Aren't you forgetting something, Johnnie?"

"What's that?" Jonetta asked, turning around to face him.

Big Louie reached into his pocket, unfolded a wad of money and peeled off a one dollar bill. He waved it in the air as if to entice her to come get it. His belly jiggled as he chuckled.

"I want to be fair, uphold our contract and call it even."

Jonetta opened the door to his office and said as loud as she could, "You can shove that dollar right up your ass!"

Jonetta was already on her third cigarette by the time she reached Midway airport. It was unusually warm for November in Chicago, so she rolled down the windows to let some of the smoke escape. None of her daughters liked that she smoked cigarettes, but of all people, Dawn couldn't complain. Jonetta was no fool. She knew that Dawn smoked "Mary Jane" for pleasure. She had been doing it recreationally since high school. But Jonetta wanted to be considerate and not have her baby girl complaining about the smoke as soon as she got in the car.

On the second time around circling the airport pick-up location, Jonetta spotted Dawn struggling with her large suitcase across the median. It looked like she packed her whole apartment in the large suitcase. Jonetta was amused and relieved that she didn't have to circle back around again. The police officer on duty was blowing the whistle and writing tickets for anyone who was not moving fast enough.

Dawn waved frantically once she spotted her blue Chrysler PT Cruiser. Jonetta honked letting her know that she saw her. As soon as a car pulled off Jonetta pulled up closer so Dawn wouldn't have to walk so far. Jonetta put the car in park and got out to greet her youngest daughter.

"Hey, baby!" Jonetta exclaimed.

"Mama!" Dawn squealed like a little girl.

They embraced and quickly put her suitcase in the trunk before the police officer walked over to harass them. Jonetta didn't want to go to jail today for cursing at a cop.

"It feels good to be home!" Dawn said, buckling her seat belt.

"Well, it looks like you packed to stay longer than four days," Jonetta replied. She glanced over at her daughter as she eased out from her parking spot.

Dawn sighed. "Yes, about that..." her voice trailed off into thought. An image of Vine giving her the peace sign on the plane popped into her mind. She was getting pissed off all over again. His ass went straight to Atlanta instead of coming to Chicago. How convenient! But there was no point in mentioning that embarrassing moment to her mother. "Well, like I mentioned before, Vine and I are breaking up. So I just packed as much as I could. Vine said that he'll just send the rest of my things later."

Jonetta nodded.

"Do you mind taking Lake Shore Drive to the house?" Dawn asked almost whining. "I miss Chicago's scenery. I just want to see the lake-front. The Hudson River pales in comparison."

"Yes, I mind taking the long route home," Jonetta snapped. "But you know I will that's why you asked."

"And can we stop for some Harold's Chicken, too?" Dawn flashed a big smile and bit her bottom lip.

"You're really pushing it! But okay," Jonetta conceded.

"So, can I stay with you and Aunt Georgia?"

"I knew that was coming, too," Jonetta replied. She kept her eyes on the road. Just the thought of all of them under one roof made her want to run to a hotel. If she would've known that Colette's apartment would catch on fire and that her brood would be living with her and Georgia, she might've battled it out with Big Louie a little bit longer.

"Well?"

"Well, it's not up to me," Jonetta continued. "But I'm sure Georgia will say yes, being the kind-hearted person that she is. And, remember, you would be staying with a house full now that Colette and the kids moved in...indefinitely."

"Oh, right," Dawn replied frowning.

"But, we'll figure something out. You're home now, with family," Jonetta said and flashed a warm smile. She patted Dawn's knee to reassure her that things will work out. Jonetta wasn't going to disappoint her baby. Dawn coming home was a good thing for Jonetta's soul, and she was happy about it.

"Thanks mama, I need to hear that," Dawn said. "I do have something else that I need to discuss with you. I was waiting until we got face-to-face to bring it up."

"You never disappoint, do you?" Jonetta asked, although she was amused by Dawn. "But, I'm listening, baby."

Dawn filled her in on the nightmares, the frequency, the old woman and a dark figure trying to smother the old lady. "I just had an episode on the plane ride here. It was so embarrassing," Dawn said, shaking her head. She searched her mother's face, but Jonetta was quiet. "So what do you think about it? Why am I a little girl in the dream? Did I go visit an old white lady when I was little? Do you think this really happened or is it just a nightmare?"

Jonetta cleared her throat. She grasped the steering wheel tighter. If she could've closed her eyes to escape in that moment she would have, but for now she had to keep her eyes on the road. Way too many questions were being thrown at Jonetta all at once. It was nearly twenty-five years ago when she took her daughters to visit her great-aunt Betty Lou. Dawn was only four-years-old at the time. There was no way she could have remembered that day. Yet, there she was inquiring about a nightmare, that was actually the last day she saw her great-aunt, Betty Lou, alive.

That old bitch was relentless until her dying day. She was still insisting that Jonetta had disowned her family, stolen her inheritance and her man. You would think that her mind would've slipped and forgot all about that, but no, not Betty Lou. Her old, withered lips just kept moving, spewing disgust and hatred for Jonetta. It's not like Jonetta asked for that life, she had no choice. But Betty Lou never saw it that way.

Betty Lou would always remind her, "We all make choices, and your choices led you here, with us. Do your duty, and earn your keep until you can do better on your own."

It was a way of life for her aunts, having men coming and going. They were proud of the brothel that they had established. It was just enough girls to keep business going that her aunts no longer had to oblige any man unless they wanted to engage. "Thunder between your thighs" is what her Aunt Adelle called it. She often told Jonetta to use her "thundering power" as often as she could to get what she wanted. It took Jonetta years to finally understand what she meant, and by then she was too tired to care.

That day Jonetta took her daughters to visit, Betty Lou just kept going on and on about all they had done for her and how she was an ingrate. Did she really expect Jonetta to be grateful for living her younger years as a prostitute? Grateful for all the men who abused and sodomized her? Grateful for never knowing what it would be like to fall in love with a man first, then give herself on her own free will? No. She wasn't grateful for that. The painful memory of it all still devastated her. It was only so much she could take.

"Earth to mama!" Dawn exclaimed.

She snapped Jonetta from her thoughts.

"Did you Google it?" Jonetta answered her finally. That's all she could think of to say. After all, Dawn did just drop a bomb on her.

"Really?" Dawn dismissed that suggestion. "I need to know why I keep having this recurring nightmare. And if it could go away that would even be better."

If it could all go away, these questions from her daughter about Betty Lou, Big Louie, the painful memories of her past, and even Dawn's nightmares. That would satisfy Jonetta just fine.

17

Colette

Once they noticed Jonetta had left for the day Georgia offered to take the children to the grocery store with her so Colette could get some peace. They had plenty of shopping to do in order to prepare for Thanksgiving dinner. Colette was eager to help cook for the family, but since her mother had cleaned thoroughly there was nothing left for her to do except wait until they came back with groceries. She figured Dawn and her mother should be arriving around the same time too.

Colette decided to put on some makeup and curl her hair. She didn't want to look like what she had just been through over the past week. Besides, Dawn was always well dressed, with flawless makeup so she wanted to impress her little sister by sprucing herself up a bit. Dawn always had presents to give everyone whenever she came to town. Colette wanted to be in a good mood for the happy occasion.

She turned on the radio to V103 and Jill Scott's voice bellowed out, "He Loves Me". A feeling of sadness swept over her. That's exactly what she wanted: a man to love her, like her, please her. All these years she wasted on Owen, loving him, like she wished he would have loved her.

Giving birth to his children, gaining weight each time, trying to make the best out of their situation, what did he think that was all for? Love. Since she's been out of the hospital, he hadn't even bothered to stop by to check on her or their children. Colette didn't expect anyone to understand, but she did miss her husband.

The house phone rang, snapping Colette from her thoughts. It was the first time she had heard the house phone ring since she had been at her aunt's house. She followed the ringing sound downstairs into the kitchen, unsure about whether or not to answer. On the fourth ring, she answered. It was Owen.

"Oh, baby, I'm so glad y'all are okay," Owen said. "I don't know what I would do if I lost my whole family in a fire." He kissed her lips repeatedly and caressed her hair.

As if Owen was reading her mind, he called to say that he wanted to visit. Of course, she was pleased to finally hear from him and since she had the house to herself, she told him to come right away.

Colette hugged him tightly when he arrived and never wanted to let go. Owen held her head in his chest for a minute, then pulled her chin up and they held each other's gaze. He held her face, kissed her forehead and gently massaged her belly. Owen was letting her know that he didn't forget what she announced as he left that day.

He sat her down on the sofa. "I'm not gonna lie, I've been missing you a whole lot," he bowed his head. "I know that I said some mean and nasty things to you last time I saw you, but I'm sorry, okay?"

Colette nodded. You also did some mean and nasty things to me, she thought to herself.

"What took you so long to come visit me?"

"I had to find the time. I'm here now and I've been thinking," Owen said, scooting closer to her. "I want my kids to grow up with their father at home. I want them to see us getting along, not fighting. I want my family back."

Colette couldn't believe what she was hearing. This was the music she wanted to hear in her ears. It made her heart glad. Maybe the fire in their apartment was a blessing in disguise. Maybe they could have a fresh start. From the beginning they had a forbidden love. Nobody approved of their marriage nor embraced Owen into the family. Colette was harshly ridiculed by her mother for choosing to marry Owen. The last thing she wanted to do was prove them all right, but over the years Owen had made it easy to do just that. Now, finally, Owen wanted to grow up, be responsible and Colette was willing to give it a try.

Colette leaned in to kiss him, and in return Owen leaned her back caressed her breasts, lifted her skirt and removed her panties. He held them up and inspected them nodding. "These are nice."

Colette giggled and blushed. She knew he would like those so she wore them just in case this very moment would happen. He pressed his thumb hard against her clitoris and moved it in a circular motion. Colette moaned in pleasure. Owen got on his knees, spread her legs wide open and began examining her like he was a gynecologist. Colette didn't say anything because she didn't want to ruin the moment, but she knew what he was doing. Owen was very protective about things he believed belonged to him and would threaten to kill anybody who thought they were entitled to his property this included Colette.

"Since when you start to go bald?"

"Since you said that you were coming by today. I wanted to be fresh for you," Colette cooed.

Seemingly satisfied by what he saw and that explanation, he began to taste her. Colette's heart raced. She panted heavily. It didn't take long for her body to shudder and tingle. She had not been touched in so long. Owen stopped just when she climaxed and examined her again.

"Look at all of that!" he exclaimed. "You really missed me, girl."

"Let's go to the bedroom," Colette suggested.

"Yeah, come on," he agreed eagerly. "Lift your skirt up so I can see that ass jiggle when you walk."

Colette obliged and Owen clasped his hands together. "Now take off your shirt, I wanna see those tits bounce up and down while you ride me."

Colette did as she was told and stood topless with her pleated skirt on.

Owen laughed, "Now you look like a naughty little school girl. I'm gonna whoop you with my big, fat ruler, bad girl." He swiftly pulled himself out of his jogging pants. He walked towards her holding himself tightly. They tongue kissed their way onto the bed. He slid his tongue slowly in and out her mouth in the same fashion as he slid himself deep inside of her.

It was like they were teenagers all over again, doing just about every position that they could think of. Owen really got excited when she climbed on top of him. He was thrusting her hips faster than she knew they could go. Their sweat stained the sheets. Finally, Colette collapsed on top of his chest. After they both caught their breath, Owen got up to clean himself off and began putting his clothes back on.

"Where are you going?" Colette asked confused. She thought that they would at least snuggle until their kids came home.

"You know I can't stay. I don't want her trippin' about me being gone too long," he explained, pulling his shirt over his head.

"What?!" Colette sat up on her elbows, blinking her eyes. She couldn't believe her ears. Did he just casually mention that side chick in their conversation?

"Shante be trippin' sometimes," he repeated. "I mean she knows why I came over here, but if I'm gone too long she'll get too suspicious. I just wanna keep the peace with her ass."

"Since when is keeping the peace with your side bitch more important than keeping the peace with your WIFE?! Besides, you haven't even seen the kids yet. They'll be home in like thirty minutes," Colette tried to reason.

"I'll be back later this week probably on Thanksgiving," Owen snapped. "Don't start nothing, Colette! I just came by to see you to show you how much I'm glad that you're okay. I'm glad to know y'all are alright. I miss you a lot, but now I have to go, alright?"

"No, it's not alright," Colette retorted. "And don't even bother coming by on Thanksgiving!" She sat up pulling the sheet up to her neck to cover her breasts. All of a sudden she felt ashamed of her nakedness. She felt used.

"Look, I already wasted an hour over here," he replied.

"Wasted?"

"We fucked for about thirty minutes. Damn! What more do you want from me? I said that I'll be back! I miss you and that good loving. It's so damn good especially when you're pregnant. And with another baby on the way, you know I'll be back sooner than later. I'm just trying to find the right time to break the news to Shante. So quit trippin' and just let me handle her!"

"Unbelievable!"

Owen walked towards her to give her a hug. "C'mon now, don't be like that. I love you, babe. I can't get enough of you even with all of our fights." He bent down to kiss her, but she pulled away. "Love you anyway."

"No!" Colette declared. "No, this isn't love."

"What?" Owen asked, apparently confused.

Colette swung her legs over the bed, wrapping the sheet around her body. She stood up and walked towards Owen so he could look her square in the eye.

"This is not the love that I had ever envisioned for myself, my children, nor for us. This is mental and physical abuse! Mind games, betrayal and lust. That's all this is, Owen."

"Oh, here you go!" He said, waving her off.

"Year after year, I have made excuses for you. I have covered up black eyes, bruises, made up lies just to protect you because I loved you. But where was my protection? Where was my love? I deserve better than this. I *want* better than this. All you do is use me for a soft spot to land when all else fails. I should be your first and only choice because I'm your wife, the mother of your children. But because women like me only see the good in our lousy husbands, and only want the best for our families by trying to keep them together, we lose sight of what we deserve too. I'm not nineteen-years-old anymore, Owen. I'm not that impressed by you anymore. You've managed to literally beat the dreams and hope for a full, happy life with my family right out of me. Thanks to the way I've allowed you to treat me I have low self-esteem, but, don't worry, I'm working on that. I've allowed you to go back and forth between me and other women when I should've left your sorry ass long time ago. It's nobody's fault but mine for who I've become, but a new day is coming. There's still hope for me. But none left for you, Owen. I'm done with this marriage."

"Done? Is that right?" He questioned, sneering at her. "Who's gonna want you with four kids and one on the way? Girl, you better take what you can get and just wait for me."

"I want me!" Colette declared. "And for now, that's all that matters."

18

This Woman's Work

All the women were busying themselves in Georgia's kitchen preparing for Thanksgiving dinner. Each assigned to a specific task as they listened to holiday music. Dawn peeled the sweet potatoes, Colette chopped celery and onions for the dressing, Phyllis cleaned the collard greens at the sink, Jonetta kneaded dough for her apple pies, and Georgia shredded blocks of cheese for the macaroni and cheese.

Phyllis bopped her head while singing to Donnie Hathaway's "This Christmas". Colette and Dawn joined in on the chorus. They were definitely in a happy moment.

"I hate to dampen anyone's mood," Jonetta said, interrupting the singing. "But, I know traditionally you girls like to go Black Friday shopping, but not this year."

"Why not?" Dawn inquired. Shopping was her favorite sport especially in Chicago.

"Because it's a protest on Black Friday," Phyllis explained. "They plan to march on Michigan Avenue and block the entrances of the stores. I don't blame them."

"Well, the protestors won't be at the malls," Colette countered.

"You can't be serious," Phyllis said incredulously. She turned the water off to face Colette. "Mama is right we're not going shopping on Friday. We have to stand in solidarity against these cops killing black lives. Besides, you don't have any money to spend anyway."

Jonetta cleared her throat. Georgia stopped shredding cheese and shot Phyllis a disapproving look.

"You know what..." Colette said. She picked up a celery stalk and threw it at Phyllis. She missed. But in return Phyllis flicked the water dripping from her hands in Colette's direction.

"That's why you missed heifer!" Phyllis sneered.

"Next time I won't!" Colette retorted. An argument with Phyllis for the holidays wasn't even worth it. Besides, it didn't matter to her whether or not she had money to spend. It was about the quality time they were spending together as sisters.

"Phyllis, be nice," Georgia chided her niece.

"That's fine. We can do something else," Dawn said and shrugged. She didn't want a war of words right before Thanksgiving.

"I just thought I'd put it out there so there wouldn't be any mis-understanding on Friday morning. And I don't want to hear of any of this talk tomorrow about Black Lives Matter, police officers, shoot-ing, protests, none of that! I don't want that as a topic of discussion at Thanksgiving. I hope that I've made myself clear."

They all avoided eye contact, but agreed. Jonetta was just being her usual, controlling self. Her daughters were used to it.

"Now, I'm going for a smoke," Jonetta announced. She placed a cheese cloth on top of her pie crust, wiped her hands on her apron and opened the back door in the kitchen.

"I'll go with you," Dawn said, dropping the knife on the counter. She quickly followed her mother outside.

Outside, Jonetta lit her cigarette and exhaled. She didn't want to be bothered with Dawn and her questions, but there she was standing next to her.

"Mama, you seemed distant yesterday after I mentioned my nightmares," Dawn began. "I don't want you thinking that I'm crazy. But I just can't help but think that something relatively close to my nightmare just may have happened in real life."

Jonetta sighed. "No, I don't think you're crazy, baby. Maybe you're just stressed."

"For three years? I don't think so, mama."

"So the nightmares started when you moved to New York?"

"Yes, at least that's as far back as I remember when they began."

"Then maybe it's a good thing you're home now, huh?"

"That's not the point, mama."

"Then what is your point, Dawn?"

"Why are you snapping at me though?"

"First of all, I smoke for enjoyment. You do know that, right?" Jonetta quipped. She pulled a long drag on her cigarette allowing the smoke to escape through her nose.

Dawn pursed her lips and tried her best not to roll her eyes at her mother. Even at thirty-years-old Dawn knew that she could still get slapped by her mother.

"Second of all, I don't have all the answers. I don't know why you're having dreams about an old white lady being smothered!" Jonetta fumed. She tossed her cigarette to the ground and stepped on it forcefully with a twist.

"Well, I took your advice last night and went on Google to find out about reoccurring dreams – "

"Spare me!" Jonetta interrupted. She headed back in the house.

"Mama, just listen," Dawn pleaded.

"Just go see a psychiatrist, Dawn!"

Jonetta walked through the kitchen and headed straight for the bathroom. Georgia watched her walk down the hallway and waited until she shut the door.

"What was that about, sugar?" Georgia asked Dawn.

"Yeah, what's up with mama?" Phyllis chimed in. "Why do you need a psychiatrist? Are you okay?"

Dawn sighed. "It's nothing." She waved her hand, not wanting to continue the conversation.

"Didn't sound like nothing to me," Colette replied. She popped a mini cinnamon roll in her mouth, waiting for Dawn to elaborate.

"Leave her alone," Georgia ordered her nieces. "If Dawn doesn't want to talk about it, that's her choice."

"Why is it that every time I opened my mouth to talk, I get chewed out?" Colette asked with her hands on her hips.

"Maybe because nobody cares about what you have to say!" Phyllis retorted. She rolled the collard greens and began cutting them, smirking at Colette. A batch was already boiling on the stove, but there never seemed to ever be enough greens for Damien's liking.

"You're just being extra sensitive, Colette," Georgia interjected, eyeing Colette carefully.

"Would you two knock it off for one night?" Dawn said. "Damn! I feel like the big sister around here."

"Language," Georgia remarked.

"Sorry, Aunty," Dawn replied.

"All these aromas are getting to me," Colette said, removing her apron. "I should check on the baby anyway. I'll be back."

"You better be back soon! We're not doing your cooking for you!" Phyllis snapped.

"Oh, stop it," Georgia admonished. "Let her get some air. We have been in here cooking for three hours now."

"We have yet to bake the cakes." Dawn pointed out. "I can soak these sweet potatoes and start on my lemon pound cake."

Georgia nodded.

Jonetta walked into the kitchen unusually quiet, avoiding eye contact with all of them. She opened the refrigerator, grabbed her bowl of apples that were mixed with cinnamon, brown sugar and lemon juice. Dawn watched her mother prepare her pie pan in admiration.

"You make the best apple pies, mama," Dawn said. She hoped that complimenting her would perk her up a bit.

"That's what they tell me," Jonetta said. She kept her hands busy and her eyes on her handiwork.

Georgia shook her head at her sister. She searched Dawn's face and saw disappointment grow across.

"Wine anyone?" Georgia asked. Whether or not they wanted a glass, Georgia was already up, headed to the wine rack.

"That would be great," Dawn replied. "What kind?"

"This is a Malbec that I picked up a while ago. Let's try it."

"Let me take a pic of it before you open it," Dawn said, reaching for her phone on the counter.

"You just want to put it on the Gram," Phyllis remarked, sneering at Dawn.

Dawn stuck her tongue out.

"None for me, though. It'll only slow me down," Phyllis said.

"Netta?" Georgia offered holding up the bottle of wine.

Jonetta shrugged. "I guess."

It was obvious that she was lost in her thoughts. Thankfully, she had prepared the apples earlier in the day; otherwise, she wouldn't be so sure everyone would be raving about this apple pie tomorrow. Since Dawn would be living with them now she knew that the subject would come up again. That caused a pinch in her chest and she gasped.

"Mama, are you alright?" Phyllis asked. She walked over towards her mother.

"I'm fine, I think it's just indigestion," Jonetta lied.

"I have antacids upstairs," Georgia offered.

Antacids were not about to cure what was bearing so heavily on Jonetta's heart. Georgia only knew some of what Jonetta had to endure. After Georgia divulged about the life that she had with Fred all these years, Jonetta stopped sharing so much with her. There's no way any of them could begin to understand the life she had to endure in this house.

19

Thanksgiving

The table had been prepared beautifully, like the kind featured in a magazine. The women of the family had outdone themselves preparing Thanksgiving dinner. They began the tradition of dressing up for Thanksgiving dinner when Fred decided to buy an expensive camera to take family photos. Even though he was not in attendance, everyone looked lovely. It would be even better if they could maintain being lovely for the remainder of the night.

Norman sat at the head of the table this year since Fred was not able to join them. Even though Norman and Jonetta haven't been together for years, he was always welcome to their holidays. It was the only guaranteed time that he would see all of them together. He was dressed nicely in an argyle brown and burnt orange sweater and neatly pressed slacks. He led the family in prayer, as always, and said a prayer for Fred. Georgia squeezed his hand tightly and thanked him for being thoughtful. They commenced to passing bowls of food around the table and eating heartily. The children had their own table with prepared plates, and Delilah was swinging peacefully.

Norman began telling them how he was going to begin frying turkeys next year, but Jonetta quickly put an end to that topic.

"Nobody wants a fried turkey, Norman," Jonetta retorted. "I think how we make our baked turkey is good enough. Wouldn't you all agree?"

"Everything tastes really good," Damien said. "God bless all the cooks."

"Yes, it does." Norman agreed quickly. "I just thought you all might enjoy something different." He shrugged and stuffed another piece of turkey breast into his mouth. He knew when to shut up.

Damien opened a bottle of Gewürztraminer and began filling up their wine glasses. "Eat, drink and be merry, everyone!"

Dawn held out her glass and thanked him as he poured.

"None for me thanks," Colette said to Damien as he tried to pour wine in her glass.

"You're not going to have some wine with us?" Phyllis inquired. "Oh, come on, girl. You can always pump and dump."

"Yes, I know," Colette replied. "I'm just not drinking, alright?"

"Well, are you on antibiotics or something? It's the holidays. Have a drink, girl! It's not like you're pregnant or anything!" Phyllis pressed the issue, trying to encourage her sister to join in on the merriment.

Colette cleared her throat. "Actually, I am."

"You're what?" Jonetta asked, dropping her fork against her plate.

"Pregnant?" Norman asked.

Colette nodded, swallowing hard. Her eyes fell to the floor. Colette clearly was embarrassed about her fifth pregnancy with Owen who was a habitual absentee husband and father.

"That's impossible!" Jonetta exclaimed, baffled by the announcement. "You said that you had your tubes tied this time."

Colette raised her eyes to meet her mothers. She straightened her back, took a deep breath and exhaled. "Well, what else did you expect me to say when you're criticizing me right after I gave birth to Delilah, mama?" She glanced over at her baby in the swing.

Jonetta's mouth flew open. "You bold faced lied to me?"

Phyllis laughed and raised her glass. "And here I was desperately trying to get pregnant and she's popping them out like a rabbit! Where's my vodka, babe?"

Damien ignored Phyllis. The last thing he wanted was his wife getting sloppy drunk on Thanksgiving. She was throwing enough digs, no need for the alcohol to start speaking on her behalf too.

"How is this even about you, Phyllis?" Colette snapped. "God, you make me sick! It's none of your business anyway."

"Actually, it's everybody's business since you can't afford to take care of your own children!" Phyllis said and got up from the table. She headed to the kitchen to look for her vodka that she brought just in case. Wine certainly was not about to do the trick for this family fiasco that was unfolding.

"Phyllis, quit starting shit!" Norman demanded.

"You're a glutton for punishment, Colette, I swear," Jonetta said, shaking her head. "Does Owen know about this?" She was fuming at this news and wanted answers.

"Of course he does, mama," Colette retorted. "He is my husband, for now, anyway."

"What the hell is that supposed to mean?" Norman probed.

"It means that I've had enough, dad." Colette confessed. She lowered her voice so her children wouldn't hear her. "I'm ready to end my marriage. Yes, even with four kids and one on the way. Regardless, I've had enough of him. I deserve better. I want a divorce."

Norman reached for his daughter's hand across the table and smiled. "Good, baby. I'm so glad to hear it. Now your breakthrough will happen. God has been waiting on you to kick that bastard to the curb. We all have!"

"Amen, Norman." Georgia agreed. "But wasn't Owen just here visiting you the other day?"

Colette shot her eyes to the floor and fidgeted in her seat.

"That's the day I told him that I wanted a divorce."

"I saw him pull off as we pulled around the corner," Georgia admitted. "He didn't even bother to wait to see his children. So I think your dad is right, sugar, sometimes God just waits on us to make a move, and then He will show us his wondrous working power. I think you're headed in the right direction. You know that you can always count on me. I'll be here to help you."

"Enough!" Jonetta shouted, slamming her hand on the table. The variety of liquids in their glasses shook. "Have you all lost your minds? All this religious talk isn't going to change Colette's harsh reality. My daughter is unemployed, uneducated, a mother of four with one on the way, with a loser of a husband who's laid up with a low self-esteem slut and you all are acting like she just said that she won the damn lottery! Am I in the fucking Twilight Zone?"

The dining room grew silent. Even the children's table got quiet.

"Jonetta, choose your words carefully in front of the children," Georgia chided. "This doesn't have to be an awful, dramatic event. Colette is sharing something with us and we need to be supportive. All the details can be discussed later."

Phyllis returned to her seat quietly, sipping from her new cocktail glass with vodka and cranberry juice. Damien shot her a disapproving look and she shot one right back, rolling her eyes.

"Well...Congratulations, sis," Dawn said and shrugged.

"Don't congratulate her on another setback!" Jonetta snapped at Dawn.

"Set back?" Colette asked her mother on the brink of tears.

"Did I stutter?" Jonetta asked and leaned across the table ready for the challenge. "Delilah just made three months old! And you have another one on the way? We're already crowded enough in this house, we can't afford another mouth to feed! You're ruining your life!" Jonetta realized that in that moment she sounded just like her mother when she found out about her unwanted pregnancy. But right now, she didn't care. This was different. It was *her* daughter.

"Mama, calm down, please," Phyllis pleaded.

"Don't you tell me to calm down!" Jonetta shouted, pointing in Phyllis's face.

Phyllis jerked her head back astonished.

"Women's voices! Women's voices! Good God almighty! Everybody pipe down!" Norman exclaimed. "Jonetta just stop it!" He was fed up with her making Colette feel bad about being pregnant all the time. He didn't like his daughter's situation either, but enough was enough.

"Stop?" Jonetta scoffed. "If you want me to stop, then maybe you need to start! Start being a father for a change. If you were around more when our girls were younger, when they really needed a father figure, maybe they wouldn't be so messed up now!"

"Messed up?" Her daughters asked simultaneously. Throats were being cleared, forks were being dropped on plates, and chatter grew over the dining room.

At the children's table all eyes were staring at the adults. Ruthie began crying and ran over to hug Colette. Lydia followed suit, hugging both her sister and mother. Phyllis rolled her eyes anticipating a chain reaction from all the kids.

"Eat your food, girls. Everything is alright, really." Serena and Sabrina just stared back at her almost in tears. "It's okay, kids, really. Go on and eat, all of you. The grown-ups are just talking."

Damien cleared his throat. "No, I think all the kids should go upstairs to watch a movie." He got up from the table not waiting on anyone's approval about his decision. "Come on kids, Uncle Damien is going to put on a good holiday movie for you upstairs." He kissed the twins on their foreheads and began leading the children upstairs.

"Good idea," Norman agreed with Damien which was rare.

"Yes, that's a good idea," Colette agreed, patting her daughters on the back. "Go with your uncle and be good."

Once they were out of sight and tempers were simmering, Georgia directed her attention to Jonetta. "When the hell are you going to put your children out of their misery?" Georgia asked slowly in a calm voice. Her eyes glowered as she stared at her sister.

They locked eyes.

"What are you talking about?" Jonetta asked.

The chatter ceased once again. They had never heard Georgia speak in such a manner to anyone. Let alone anyone speak that way towards their mother. They all shifted uncomfortably in their seats.

"I am *so* sick of you," Georgia declared, determined to get her point across. She exhaled and continued to glare at her sister.

"You're sick of me?" Jonetta placed her hand on her chest as if she were innocent and shocked by Georgia's bold statement. She looked back and forth between everyone at the table in dismay.

Georgia continued to glare at Jonetta.

"Have you had too much to drink?" Jonetta asked her sister.

"This is my house and I'm speaking! So you just shut up and listen!" Georgia demanded, annoyed that Jonetta wanted to play dumb. She had everyone's full attention. "All this time I've seen you play everyone like it's a chess game. I'm used to it. I grew up with you and watched you manipulate everyone around you until you chased them all away. Even the way you manipulated your way into my house. Would you care to tell everyone here the real reason you *had* to move into my home? The truth will come to light anyway whether you are prepared to accept it or not. Your past is anything but righteous. This is a chance for you to relate to your daughter instead of acting like you're holier than thou! You've been given plenty of opportunity to make up for it, but instead, you pile shit on top of more shit and dowse it with molasses thinking nobody will notice the stench, but I do. Oh, yes, I smell it and it's rotten! It's time to clean it up Jonetta Mae! This is real life here. You're toying with real people, your children, their emotions, and livelihood. What you say and do has a ripple effect on your daughters, but you're too caught up in trying to save face and putting on appearances that you can't see it. Your daughters deserve better from their mother. I wish that God would've allowed me to become a mother. I will never understand why He would give someone like you so many beautiful gifts when all you do is take them for granted and misuse them. You don't deserve these blessings, but yet, you have them. Your daughters come to you for guidance, truth and advice and all you do is spew bitterness, deceit and malice." Georgia fumed. "For once in your life tell them the truth!"

Jonetta mashed her lips together and glared at Georgia. Her whole body stiffened and she was barely breathing. The pinch in her chest returned, but she managed not to flinch this time.

"The truth about what?" Dawn asked looking back and forth between her mother and Georgia. Damien came back from getting the kids settled and slid into his chair quietly. He touched Phyllis's knee, but she jerked away.

Jonetta exhaled and closed her eyes. She swallowed hard and opened her eyes. Every set of eyes at the table were glued to her.

"The truth, huh? You want the truth from me?" Jonetta snapped.

"It'll set you free, I promise, Netta," Georgia replied, placing a napkin delicately in her lap. "Give it a try!"

"They wouldn't even begin to understand..."

"Try us," Norman said gently. He leaned on the table resting on his elbows. Being married to Jonetta had not been easy. Norman knew that he didn't know everything there was to know about Jonetta so he was waiting patiently to hear what she had to say.

Jonetta shot him a look across the table. The last thing she wanted to do during Thanksgiving dinner was confess about her past sins. But here they were waiting on baited breath, staring with anticipation. They were not giving her much choice.

"We grew up poor in a small Pennsylvania town. I was determined and desperate to get out of there. One day I stole Georgia's peach frolic dress, trying to get attention of some of the well-to-do men in town. But instead, I was raped by a neighbor and became pregnant at seventeen-years-old."

"Wait a minute," Georgia interrupted. "That's the first I'm hearing of this, Netta! Our neighbor? Who? Paul King?"

Jonetta nodded.

"I tried explaining that to our mother, but she didn't want to hear it. Instead, she sent me up here to live with her two aunts, Betty Lou and Adelle. I cleaned this very house for them. One day I took a stumble down those basement stairs. I broke my leg and lost the baby. It was a boy. He was buried in the backyard, or so I thought. Once I healed my great aunts had a new job for me. They took me shopping for fine clothes and lingerie, combed my hair, put make up on me, sprayed expensive perfume on me and made me earn my keep. Right here in this house."

"Earn your keep?" Dawn asked confused.

"The men came and went," Jonetta continued. "But there was one man in particular who took a liking to me, Mr. Lucky. Only thing was, my Aunt Betty Lou had already been in a relationship with him. I didn't know it. He did, but didn't care. Once Betty Lou found out, we fought, right there in the kitchen. I left and moved in with him. Things were going just fine for us until one night he offered me up to his friend as his birthday gift. After that awful night, Mr. Lucky became my pimp. I had nowhere to go, so I stayed until... until he died."

"How did he die, Jonetta?" Georgia probed for the sake of everyone listening. She already knew the answer to that question.

"A stroke," Jonetta answered. "The doctors ruled his death alcohol poisoning and he had high blood pressure which caused the stroke. I kept putting drinks in his hand all night long. I wasn't proud of what I did. It may have contributed to his death, but I'll never know. I was desperate. I didn't even have a plan. I just wanted him drunk enough so I could leave. After he died, I was all alone for sure in this big city. I was on bad terms with my aunts, but I had the house. Betty Lou wanted the house and all of the jewelry and furs, but I refused. I kicked out all the extra girls that Mr. Lucky kept coming and going. I got a job at the post office where I met your father. He was dropping off a package one day and we locked eyes and well... that was that. When you girls were little we fell on hard times thanks to your father's gambling habits."

Norman hung his head.

"We broke up eventually. Times were really rough back then. So, I visited Betty Lou out of desperation to ask for any financial assistance she could give, and to find out if my mother or Aunt Adelle had left any inheritance for me," Jonetta admitted. "I took you all with me, remember? It was during that visit she told me what she did to my son. I thought that he was buried in the yard underneath the mulberry tree all those years. She confessed, nearly on her death bed, that she threw him in the trash. My great-aunt Betty Lou had thrown my stillborn son *in the trash*. Family! Then she had the nerve to laugh wickedly about it. That was it! I saw red. I grabbed a pillow and tried to smother the old bitch. But I heard a noise, and turned around to see Dawn standing in the hallway. My baby girl."

Jonetta locked eyes with Dawn and bit her bottom lip. In that moment, she felt really guilty about dismissing Dawn's concerns about her nightmares.

"I grabbed you girls and left this house," Jonetta continued. "So, Dawn, those are the recurring nightmares that you keep having. It's probably a suppressed memory and I regret that terribly."

"Well, did you really kill her, mama?" Dawn asked just above a whisper.

"No, baby, I didn't. I think only because God sent you down that hallway at that very moment to stop me from what would've been a tragic crime. She passed away naturally a few weeks later. I didn't attend the funeral and that's when I called Georgia."

Dawn sat back in her chair and folded her arms. "So you were willing to let me think that I was crazy? And you even suggest that I see a psychiatrist, mama!"

"I'm sorry, baby." Jonetta apologized. "You came out of nowhere and just dropped a bomb on me. I didn't want to talk about it. It's painful."

"So what the hell does that have to do with why you're living here, again?" Norman asked.

"A few months ago, the birthday boy from that awful night, showed up at my doorstep. He was convinced that Mr. Lucky owed him a debt and it was up to me to pay it. Of course, I told him to kiss it where the sun doesn't shine, but he was persistent. He told me the house would be good enough to cover the debt. After weeks of harassing me, I finally agreed. I sold the house to him for a dollar. That's why I officially moved in here with Georgia."

A moment of silence passed.

"My God, Jonetta," Norman replied, breaking the silence. "I had no idea. You've never mentioned any of this to me before."

"I didn't want you to know that you were marrying a whore," Jonetta confessed. "I'm sorry." Her voice cracked and she grabbed a napkin from the table to catch her tears that escaped without her permission. She was so embarrassed that she stood up to leave. It was too much to have all of them staring at her. Now they knew the part of her life that she so desperately tried to conceal.

Norman rushed to her side, "No, no baby, not at all. You were a victim who was just trying to survive. It must turn your stomach living in this house again."

Jonetta nodded. They hugged each other briefly.

"We'll think of something," Norman said, comforting her. "Now tell me who this son-of-a-bitch is and where I can find him."

"No," Jonetta replied, wiping her nose. "It's just as well. It's so much better this way. Trust me. Besides, I made him put a clause in the papers that if he so much as contacts me the contract will be null and void."

"Wow! So you were a prostitute?" Colette scoffed. "My mother, who is above reproach and so critical of everyone, was a prostitute! That's some nerve, mama."

Norman shot Colette a disapproving look.

"I need another drink," Phyllis said.

"I need a cigarette," Jonetta said.

"No. All of you need Jesus!" Georgia proclaimed.

"Look, we are a family," Norman declared. He helped Jonetta back in her seat and touched the side of her face. "We have to stop behaving like enemies all the time. I know that I was not the best father or husband. I'm truly sorry for the pain that I've caused. I see now that my absence had an effect on all of you. I can only ask for your forgiveness. You're my family. You're all that I have left in this world and I love you all. Enough with all the secrets, okay? Look at how many years of pain your mother has carried around. Secrets will kill us on the inside."

"Your father is right, girls," Jonetta admitted, patting his hand. "We have to do better."

They were all silent.

Jonetta continued, "Colette, I'm sorry. I don't ever want you to feel that you have to lie to me because I can't handle your truth. I feel so terrible that I've made you feel bad about yourself or having children. I just wanted better for you. But I love my grandchildren. I'm here to help you, too, baby. You know that I love you."

Colette wiped away tears streaming down her face and nodded. "I know, mama. I know."

"We all love you, Colette," Norman said sincerely. He bent down to give her a warm hug. Colette embraced her father and released him with a big smile on her face. She needed that reassurance coming from her father that everything would work out just fine.

Norman walked around the table towards Damien and Phyllis. He felt that the time was right to clear the air with everyone.

"Damien, now, what you're gonna do is go to a gambler's anonymous meeting to get some help."

Jonetta gasped. "A gambler's what? What in the hell?"

"Dad, how did you know?" Phyllis asked.

"Well, sweetheart, Damien is not the only one who had some bad habits as a young man. I figured if it wasn't drugs or drinking or women, it had to be something else this man was spending his money on. I made a call to one of my old buddies and asked him to check in some of the gambling spots where we used to hang out. Sure enough, he saw Damien there just last week."

"Last week?" Phyllis shrieked. She looked back and forth between her dad and husband. It took everything in Phyllis not to pop Damien in the back of his head in front of everybody. All she could muster was a nasty snarl on her face and clenched fists.

Damien leaned back in his chair and folded his arms. His eyes narrowed and lips grew tight. He clenched his teeth so rapidly that his jaw bones and temples were visibly pulsating.

"So now you're spying on me?" Damien asked in disbelief. "You could've just come to me, man-to-man, instead of putting my business out here like this. Damn! Y'all really know how to turn sugar to shit real quick!"

Norman raised his hands in defense. "Now before you go getting all riled up, I did it for your own good. You're not a bad guy, Damien. My daughter loves you and so do those beautiful twins. You've been in our family for years, and we love you. But you need some professional help. You think you can do this on your own, but you can't. Trust me. I had a thing for the horses. Gambling is a tough, bad habit to kick. You need help and I'm here to help."

"I didn't ask for your help!" Damien declared. "Last week, I just needed one more hit to get us back on our feet. To pay back debts, including the one we owe you. Don't you want your money back?"

"Damien, you promised me that you would stop gambling," Phyllis said through clenched teeth. Her cheeks were flushed from embarrassment.

Norman waved her off. "Promises are easily made and easily broken. It's time you grow the hell up! Your husband has an addiction, and it won't be resolved by making promises." Satisfied that Phyllis got the message, he turned his attention to Damien. "Of course, I want my damn money back, but not at the expense of you getting into deeper debt, son. I have a number you can call and if you're not comfortable with that, I can be your sponsor. Just think about it."

"Well, if I have to get some help, then you do too," Damien said, looking at Phyllis. "You drink too much. So if you're ready, then I'm ready." He took the glass from Phyllis's hand and placed it on the table.

Phyllis's mouth flew open in disbelief.

Damien nodded confirming that he meant it. "You're not fooling anybody with those water bottles, babe."

"Who are you people?" Dawn asked, looking around the table. "Just when you think you know your own family, y'all come out of the woodworks with secrets, on Thanksgiving no less!"

"Who are we? We are your family!" Phyllis replied indignant. "Like it or not, Dawn, we're not perfect and neither are you. I'm sure that you have more than enough skeletons just waiting to fall out of your closet. All those comments on your social media pages, full of innuendos are a dead giveaway that you lead an alternative life. Mama may think you're a goody-two-shoes, but you're not fooling me! No matter how far away you try to run, you can't change who you really are and where you came from. Wherever you go, there you are!"

"Welcome home," Damien said.

"Well, Dawn won't be running any time soon. Will you, baby?" Jonetta interjected, always coming to Dawn's defense. She gave Dawn a nod for approval to share her news with the family.

Dawn's eyes widened and she sucked her teeth. "Gee, thanks mama!" She cleared her throat, raising her glass of wine. "Well, since we're all sharing and clearing the air. I'm here to stay. There. I said it."

"Really?" Colette asked with a huge smile on her face. "The kids will be thrilled to have their aunty back home."

"That's interesting," Phyllis remarked.

The doorbell rang and Dawn was relieved for the interruption. Georgia looked at Jonetta and Jonetta shrugged her shoulders. She wasn't expecting anyone. Georgia excused herself to open the door. The conversation continued about Dawn returning home for good until she figured out her next move.

"Vine and I broke up," Dawn admitted, shrugging her shoulders. "So here I am."

"Oh, I'm so sorry, hunny," Colette replied. "I really thought he was the one for you."

"I am," Vine said. He stood in the entryway with his eyes glued on Dawn.

"Vine!" Dawn exclaimed. She leaped from her seat bumping the dining room table, spilling a few drinks. Dawn ran to hug him, tightly locking her fingers together behind his neck. Tears spilled down her face onto his navy pea coat.

"We're going to straighten things out," Vine said softly and kissed her forehead. "You know I love you, girl."

"Come on in, son," Norman said. "We have an extra chair waiting on you."

"There's enough room for anyone who wants to be part of this family," Georgia said.

"That's right." Jonetta agreed with her sister. "We won't ever be perfect, but we are family."

Acknowledgments

I am most grateful and thankful to God, my Creator, for leading me to this point of following my dream and embracing my natural talents. It was a long road that led me to finally find the courage to find my own voice. To my family and close friends, I would like to say thank you for your patience. I've been talking about publishing a novel for years, and finally, it has come to fruition. To my daughters, Lexy and Nadia, you may not know it, but you are my inspiration to continue to evolve and achieve goals. One day you will understand the sacrifice, time and dedication it took to accomplish this lifelong dream. Stick to your dreams and work hard to make them come true. Follow your own path, girls!

To my literary mentors, RM Johnson and Mary Monroe thank you for your guidance during my journey. Your literary careers inspired me and you were gracious enough to provide insight to help me along the way. To Justin Q. Young, my graphic designer and advisor, thank you for having patience with me during this process. I truly appreciate all of your seeds of knowledge that you planted to ensure my growth. You are the definition of the new Renaissance Man. To my pilot readers, thank you for being available to read chapters, give feedback, and encouragement. This wasn't easy, but I knew you were rooting for me so I couldn't let you down.

To my new readers, thank you for giving me a chance to sweep you into another world, time and space. I want to hear from you. I hope you enjoy the characters as much as I did creating them for you.
It's always love,
Rebekah S. Cole

Email: beckywrites2@gmail.com
Facebook: www.facebook.com/rebekahscole
Instagram: www.instagram.com/rebekahscole
Twitter: @rebekahScole
#womensvoices

Book Club Questions

1. The first chapter opens with Jonetta ridiculing her middle daughter, Colette, for having another baby. Do you think she had a choice in her marriage, considering her circumstances?

2. Abuse comes in all forms. Can a man truly rape his wife? Why do you think Colette stayed with Owen for so long? If you know a 'Colette' in your life, what would you advise her/hope for her? Is there any hope for Owen to change his ways?

3. Jonetta was not the traditional mother, by far. How do you think her behavior affected her three daughters? Do you think if Jonetta dealt with her demons long ago that her daughters would've chosen different paths? If so, in what way?

4. The mother-daughter relationship can be fragile at times. What do you think Jonetta could've done differently for each of her daughter's dilemmas in this story?

5. Likewise, the father-daughter relationship can be fragile as well. Norman admits that he could have done better in the past. Do you think he deserves forgiveness from his daughters? Did the behavior of Jonetta keep him away?

6. How do you feel about the marriages in this family? Do you think any of them will last/worth the work? Do you think women have the tendency to push their husbands out of the picture, but play the victim instead?

7. Is Phyllis an alcoholic like her husband, Damien, claims? Or does she just need something to take the edge off of stressful situations? What other method could she practice to reduce stress?

8. Can Damien quit gambling on his own? Should Phyllis go back to work to help with the household bills?

9. Georgia and Phyllis, aunt and niece, both struggled with infertility. In a family of women sometimes there are "fertile Myrtles" and sometimes there are infertile women. Do you think this caused jealousy in the sister dynamic: Georgia/Jonetta and Phyllis/Colette?

10. Dawn is a free-spirited, childless, ambitious young woman. Do you think she should consider being more stable/settled if that's what her boyfriend, Vine, is expecting? What are your thoughts on her recreational drug use and promiscuity?

11. Georgia was always talking about God and taking the high road. How do you feel about how she confronted her sister, Jonetta, at the dinner?

12. We all know that the best kept secret is the one you never tell. But secrets can also be a burden to carry, having an effect on your spirit and your family. After reading this novel, do you feel compelled to deal with your family secrets? Or are they best left unspoken?

About the Author

Rebekah S. Cole is a Chicago native who grew up in a large family and began writing short stories and poetry as an escape. At an early age her grandmother introduced her to poetry readings at the local library. As poetry readings became popular among young adults, Rebekah recited her poetry at several locations across the city. She then began taking a stab at writing novels. But as life would have it, motherhood, enrolling into college and a budding finance career took precedent over her first love. However, her passion for creative writing and publishing a novel was still in the back of her mind.

In between her demanding schedule, Rebekah served as a panelist at the 2011 Black Women's Expo in Chicago, IL discussing women's issues with self-image. She was also a first place poetry winner for Women's History Month and a contributing editor for her company newsletter and has attended writing workshops.

After achieving another life goal, earning a Bachelor of Arts Degree, Rebekah returned to her creative writing skills and completed her debut novel, *Women's Voices*.

Made in the USA
Charleston, SC
15 April 2016